Wondrous and Perilous™ Adventures

Furvik's Destiny

Adam Dreece

For old-school style fantasy role playing games
B/X, 1e, 2e

CREDITS

Writer: Adam Dreece, **Editors**: Aerin Caley, Jess Alter, Mike Bybee **Cover Art:** Joey Docil **OSR Logo:** Jennifer Zouak - Jen's RPG Art **Interior Image & Illustration Artists**: Joey Docil, Jessica Lamb, Gabe Fua, iStockPhoto.com / enviromantic /DavidGoh, Rick Hershey - Empty Room Studios, Publisher's Choice Quality Stock Art © Rick Hersey / Fat Goblin Games –used with permission

Map Artist: Megan Beaudoin

Beta Readers & Play testers: Josh Pix, Ryan Wynne, Zimzimdar, Tyler Powell, Mark Gottselig

A Huge Thank You to Christopher Clark for the mentoring, advice, next level beta-reading, and encouragement. Completely unexpected and very deeply appreciated.

COPYRIGHT

ADZO Publishing Inc. Waterloo, Ontario Canada contact@adzopublishing.com

First printing, electronic version 1.0.16

ISBN - PDF 978-1-988746-47-0 Paperback 978-1-988746-48-7 Hardcover 978-1-988746-49-4

TABLE OF CONTENTS

About this Adventure

Welcome to the *Wondrous & Perilous*™ *Adventure - Furvik's Crypt*. It is designed for 3-6 characters of levels 5-7 and should take a few gaming sessions to get through.

WHAT YOU NEED TO PLAY

This adventure requires an old-school gaming system like Old-School Essentials, Castles and Crusaders, OSRIC, Basic Fantasy, or a similar B/X, 1e, or 2e system. It is not a stand-alone book.

For simplicity, the book uses the term Game Master (GM), rather than any other term, like referee, to refer to the person running the game - that crazy, marvelous, story-weaver of a person.

SUGGESTIONS AND THE GM's CALL

For those that need it to be said, here it is. The decision of whether or not an item has a certain power, whether the power can work as written, etc. is entirely the GM's call.

Everything in this book is a suggestion and is not intended to detract from the story, flow of play, or make anyone regret committing time to this great game.

Being a GM is like having homework in creative writing and accounting so that you can try and deliver a live presentation to hecklers who are hopefully on your side. I have mad respect for anyone up for running a game, so it is always their final call in my books.

MAPS

The adventure includes a numbered map, for the GM, and a players Map (without the numbers) near the back of the adventure.

CHECKS, STATS, AND MORE

Feel free to jump into the adventure, but if you're not familiar with creature stat blocks or you're using a system that's not necessarily 100% compatible with Old School game mechanics, read on.

ABILITY CHECKS AND DIFFICULTY

There are points in the adventure where it's proposed to have an ability check. Note that this is a suggestion and you, as GM, can decide what fits the narrative better.

Depending on the system you are using, it may use a Roll-Under approach (like 1e) or a Difficulty Class (DC) (like 5e) or something else. In order to keep things as simple and compatible as possible, you'll find a table of suggested modifiers for the different levels of difficulty below. Note that if an encounter doesn't explicitly state the difficulty, it means it's medium.

Difficulty	Target or bonus/penalty to attempt
Easy	DC8 or +2 bonus
Medium	DC12 or no bonus/penalty
Hard	DC16 or -2 penalty
Very Hard	DC20 or -4 penalty

CREATURES

The adventure includes many creatures, including some new takes on existing creatures. In every encounter there is a simple, summary stat block provided. If the creature is a new creature, or a new take, the details are provided at in the section entitled *Creatures*, in the back of the adventure.

UNDERSTANDING THE STAT BLOCK

In every encounter, a stat block is given for the creatures. Sometimes there is treasure explicitly mentioned and sometimes, if the treasure type is listed (TT), roll for it in your GM's guide.

Creature abilities for new creatures are listed at the end of the stat block (Abilities) with details provided in the *Creatures* section.

Here's an example stat block with explanations for each part.

Sample Creature

*AC 6[14], HD 3+1 (13hp), Att 1x Short Sword (1d6), MV 120'
(40'), SV D13 W14 P13 B16 S15 (Thief 1), ML 8, AL Neutral Evil,
XP 10, NA 1d8 (3d10), TT U, Abilities: A, B, C*

- **AC 6[14]** Descending Armor Class is shown first and is for systems that use the classic lookup tables for the target to hit or uses THAC0 (see below). The number in brackets is for systems that use Ascending Armor class.

- **HD 3+1 (13hp)** This is the creature's Hit Dice, i.e. what level it is and how many d8s it has for potential hit points. If there is an additional number, like the +1 in this case, that's the number of additional hit points added to the total - so if 12 had been rolled, 1 would be added, giving 13. For convenience, a suggested number of hit points is included in brackets. You can use that or roll for the creature.

- **Att 1x Short Sword (1d6)** Attack shows how many attacks the creature has per round as well as the type of weapon and the damage. In this example, the creature uses a sword, rather than claws or a bite, and the attack does 1d6 damage.

- **MV 120' (40')** Movement has two numbers. The first (120') is how many feet the creature can move as its base movement rate. The second (40') shows the number of feet the creature can move, on its turn, in combat. Usually, the base movement rate is 3x the encounter rate.

- **THAC0 18 [+1]** To-Hit-Armor-Class-Zero provides a quick way to be able to determine what the creature needs to roll to hit an Armor Class of 0 (shown as 18) instead of needing to look at the classical attack matrix. This is for classic descending Armor Class rules. For ascending AC, use the number in the brackets (+1).

- **SV D13 W14 P13 B16 S15 (Thief 1)** These are the creature's saving throws, provided so you don't have to look them up. D is for the Death/Poison saving throw, W is for Wand, P for Paralysis, B for Breath Weapon, and S for Spells. If you want to use the charts in your system, use the information in the parentheses at the end, for example Thief 1.

- **ML 8** This is the creature's morale rating.

- **Al Neutral Evil** This is the creature's alignment. If you are playing a B/X style game, ignore the Evil/Good part.

- **XP 10** This shows how many experience points (XP) besting a single creature of this type is worth. That could mean killing them, sneaking past them, etc., as determined by you, the GM.

- **NA 1d8 (3d10)** Number Appearing shows you how many you are likely to find wandering around, in this case 1d8. The number in the

parentheses shows how many would be found in a lair, encampment, or group. In this example, that'd be 3d10.

- **TT U (A)** This tells you what treasure table to use for the creature from your GM's guide, like the Old-School Essentials, the Advanced Fantasy: Referee's Tome. The first letter, U, indicates what treasure table to use for the individual creature. If there's a letter in brackets, that's the treasure type for any lair, encampment, or if there is a significant number of the creatures.

- **Abilities**: This section summarizes any special abilities that the creatures have. To get the full description and details, you should look up the creature either in the GM creature guide of your system or in the *Creatures* section at the back of the adventure, if they are a new or variant creature.

- **Items:** If the creature has a magical weapon, like a club +1 or a magical shield, those bonuses have not been applied to the creature's ability to hit or take damage as shown. The reason being the creature could be disarmed or the item somehow taken away from them. Remember to include the item bonuses if the creature is using the items.

MAGICAL ITEMS

This adventure includes new magical items which are mentioned in the encounter in which they can be found and have a reference such as (See *Magical Items*) to indicate where you can get the details about the item. If there is no such reference, it's a common item and should be included in your system's GM guide, like the *Old-School Essentials Advanced Referee's Guide*.

Some of the new items are from *Wondrous & Perilous*™ *Treasures Volume 1* or *Volume 2*, and others may well find themselves in a future volume.

Hook

A close family member of one of the party members was killed when they tried to prevent the theft of a powerful magical item from a local, secret temple called the Gauntlets of the Ice Demon Kofnar. The temple leader has asked for help before the items power can be unlocked and unspeakable evil unleashed.

The party could be motivated by any, or all, of the following:

- Revenge for the family member or close friend
- Restoring honor to a sacred temple
- Desire to stop an unknown evil from being unleashed

It's up to you as GM to determine what type of close friend or family member works best for the party - brother, sister, father, mother, cousin, aunt, uncle, etc. Wherever you see [Family Member] in the text, swap it out for whatever you decide.

GM Background

TEMPLE AND THE GAUNTLETS

Hidden in the forest near a small town the party find themselves is a temple that has been secretly responsible for guarding different magical items over the many years it had been there. Most recently, it was the *Gauntlets of the Ice Demon Kofnar* (see *Magical Items*) which was being hidden there until it could be safely transported and destroyed.

The half-dozen members of the temple provide medical services for those in the town when needed in exchange for deliveries of food, blankets, and such.

The family member was delivering food to the temple when the attack happened.

FURVIK AND THE EVIL SPIRIT

Furvik is a goblin sorcerer who for a long time was a second-rate hireling of various bandit and other groups. Often mistreated or cheated out of what was owed to him, one day after helping a group of bandits ambush adventures who'd looted a crypt, Furvik heard a voice and felt a presence. It helped him slay the bandits when they tried to turn on him and a year later, become the leader of the Ogre Cult.

No one has heard or seen the mysterious Evil Spirit, other than Furvik. It has made him believe it is a long forgotten god and given him a taste of power. Furvik believes that with the power of the gauntlets unlocked, he'll become the living avatar of the forgotten god.

He has led the cult members to believe it will grant them all significant power, making them titans. The truth, known only to the Evil Spirit, is that it will allow it make Furvik stronger and possess him, while consuming the life of the ogres.

No explicit origin or name is given to the Evil Spirit to allow you, as GM, to connect it to another adventure if you'd like. Otherwise, it is simply not known.

KOKEEN AND THE OGRE CULT

The ogre cult is led by a highly honorable high-priest, Kokeen, who follows Furvik reluctantly. A year and a half ago, to the astonishment of all of the ogres, Furvik defeated Kokeen in ritual combat.

Kokeen's slowly been accepting that Furvik is what he says he is as he has found them a new home (the crypt), made them all stronger (sharing some of the evil spirit's power, resulting in Blessed Ogres), led them to start attaining wealth (through successful raids), now is on the verge of giving them all tremendous power through a ritual to release the magic within the gauntlets.

That all said, Kokeen feels there's something amiss. She has a very deeply rooted sense of justice and it wouldn't take much to tip her over the edge to standing by while the party does what they need to.

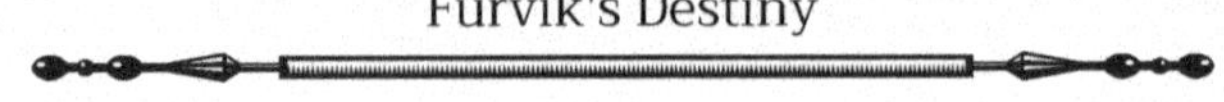

ABOUT THE CRYPT

THE CRYPT

On the far side of town that was once devastated by a mysterious fire, is an overgrown, forgotten small cemetery. At the far end, hidden by twisted and snarled trees is a small mausoleum for a once famous, but long since forgotten, sorcerer. This is where the Evil Spirit led Furvik and revealed a secret door that led to the crypt underneath which has become the lair for Furvik and the ogre cult.

The few townspeople who have seen things going on know better than to say anything as those who have seem to have gone missing.

The crypt has a wide entrance and passages, 10', and its ceilings are high, at least 15'. It is filled with traps and puzzles which the Evil Spirit has helped Furvik and the ogres avoid.

KEYS, SECRET PASSAGES, AND TRAPS

Upon entering the crypt, there are three doors with the party intended to go through the eastern most first, find a lever, then go into beyond the middle door, find another lever, and then finally the western most door.

Furvik and his lieutenants have crypt keys which unlock secret doors and deactivate (or activate) traps. They have all memorized where they are. The party should not come into possession of a working crypt key too early as it could bypass a large part of the adventure. Feel free to have any keys found too early break when used.

The secret doors are particularly hard to find and should have a penalty applied to trying to find them (see *Ability Checks & Difficult*).

LIGHT IN THE CRYPT

Most of the crypt is completely dark as Furvik and the ogres have been granted magical dark vision from the Evil Spirit. The party needs to provide their own source of light. The crypt seems to eat up the light, making magical lighting last half as long and cutting the range of infravision, and similar abilities and effects, by half.

While Furvik and the ogres have been given magical dark vision, they can see where there's light. This allows them to tell where there are intruders and avoid stepping into the light accidentally.

Poison Pit Traps

The crypt has many hidden poison pit traps. Some of the pits, like those in Area 2, only become active after the lever in Area 3 is pulled.

Unless the Area description says otherwise, the pits have a small, jagged ledge on one side which a thief or rogue-type can discover with a successful Find Traps attempt. A failed attempt could either indicate the wrong side as having the ledge. For any character in medium or heavy armor, consider requiring an easy dexterity check or requiring the assistance of someone to

navigate the ledge. Note that Furvik and the ogres have memorized where all of the ledgers are and how to get around the pits.

All of these poison pit traps, except for the extra-large one in Area 20, are covered with a seemingly solid cover which gives away and hides when 20 pounds or more is applied to it.

Falling into the spike-covered pit causes 1d8 damage and requires a Save vs Poison. Failing the save results in sluggishness and stupor in the form of -1 to strength, dexterity, and wisdom for 10 minutes.

During those 10 minutes, if the character becomes poisoned again, the effects compound and restarts the 10-minute timer. For example, Tomsum falls into the first pit and fails their save. They have a -1 to their strength, dexterity, and wisdom. Nine minutes later, they fall into a second pit and fail the Save vs Poison. Now they have -2 to those stats for the next ten minutes.Unfortunately, Tomsum falls into a third pit nine minutes later, fails their save again, and now have a -3 penalty to their stats for the next ten minutes.

If any stat drops below 3, the character falls into a coma for 1d6 hours and awakens free of the poison.

Getting out of a pit trap alone is treacherous, never mind that the cover folds back into place after 2 rounds. To get out with help does not require any form of check. However, to get out without the aid of someone requires a dexterity check (see *Ability Checks and Difficulty*).

Setting the Stage

Create a narrative for the players from the following points:

- The party comes to this small, busy trading town so one (or more) of the party can visit [Family Member] whom they haven't seen in quite some time.

- Word was sent ahead for [Family Member] to meet the party at the tavern. They are very late. The party has asked around, but no one has seen [Family Member] in several hours.

- The party has heard a few rumors about the place and surrounding.

- The party has a bad feeling, and any divine-type characters (Clerics, Paladins, etc.) can feel the hint of an evil presence in the general area.

RUMORS

While waiting for [Family Member], the players will have heard 1d4+2 rumors. *True (T) - False (F)*

1. There's an ogre cult in the area that serves a new master, a small master. He has somehow made the cult members stronger than regular ogres. (T).

2. A cult lives in a trap-filled dungeon nearby. Somehow, they get around without any problems. (T)

3. There's a nasty blood poison about. At first, it makes you wobbly and loopy before it paralyzes and kills you. The only way to be rid of it is with a twisted divine harming spell. (F)

4. [Family Member] was doing something suspicious lately, sorry to say. They were seen heading out into the woods with supplies. (F)

5. Some adventurers were passing through, and dropped a sheet with old symbols them. They meant different things - one meant pull, one push, another turn. (T - give +1 to intelligence check when trying to figure out symbol puzzles in the crypt).

6. I think the elder of the temple is hiding a lot more than he lets on. Probably part of some cult. (F)

7. I heard there were some adventurers hired by the mayor, a few weeks ago, to investigate that crypt. That was before the mayor went missing. No one knows what happened. I don't get how that many people could fit into that tiny crypt though. (T)

8. There are ogres about who can see in complete darkness, as if they had magical eyes. (T)

9. There are ogre zombies walking about. (F)

10. An adventurer passed through a few months ago, shaken to the core. Taking about evil furniture and teeth, so many teeth. (T)

11. If you meet the ogre priestess Kokeen, talk with her. Smart, grounded, unlike any other ogre in these parts. (T)

12. The great hero Solonark was said to have been buried here, long, long ago. Sad tale, a slave transformed to hero and then king. His queen died in childbirth, leaving him with one son who was soon assassinated by a neighboring kingdom. It broke him. Turned him to darkness. (T)

Start

Here's what happens:

- The Family Member staggers into the tavern, covered in blood and hitting the floor hard.

- A party member gets to [Family Member] in time to hear them say, "Ogres attacked the temple. Please, make it right. Help the elder. Outside."

- The Family Member dies, unable to be healed from their wounds. They have nothing of use in their possession.

- Everyone in the tavern is stunned, no one has anything helpful to say.

Outside, the party finds the temple elder slumped over on a horse, badly injured, but he will live. The elder shares the following with the party:

- The temple was guarding a powerful magical item called the *Gauntlets of the Ice Demon Kofnar* (see *Magical Items*). After six months of waiting, they were preparing to send it for destruction this afternoon when they were attacked.

- Ogres, led by a goblin spellcaster, attacked and took the gauntlets. The goblin leader said something about unlocking its power and they were to return to the crypt.

- The elder knows they have been hiding out in the crypt, the rumors about a level below it being true.

- He asks the party to avenge the death of [Family Member] and to return the gauntlets. A reward of 20,000 gp is offered.

- Once the party agrees, the elder teleports the party to the entrance of the crypt.

- The elder passes out and the tavern owner offers to take care of him.

Time is of the essence. If the party attempts to return to town to get provisions, or rest up, they will fail the mission. However, you're the GM, you can decide what fits best.

Map

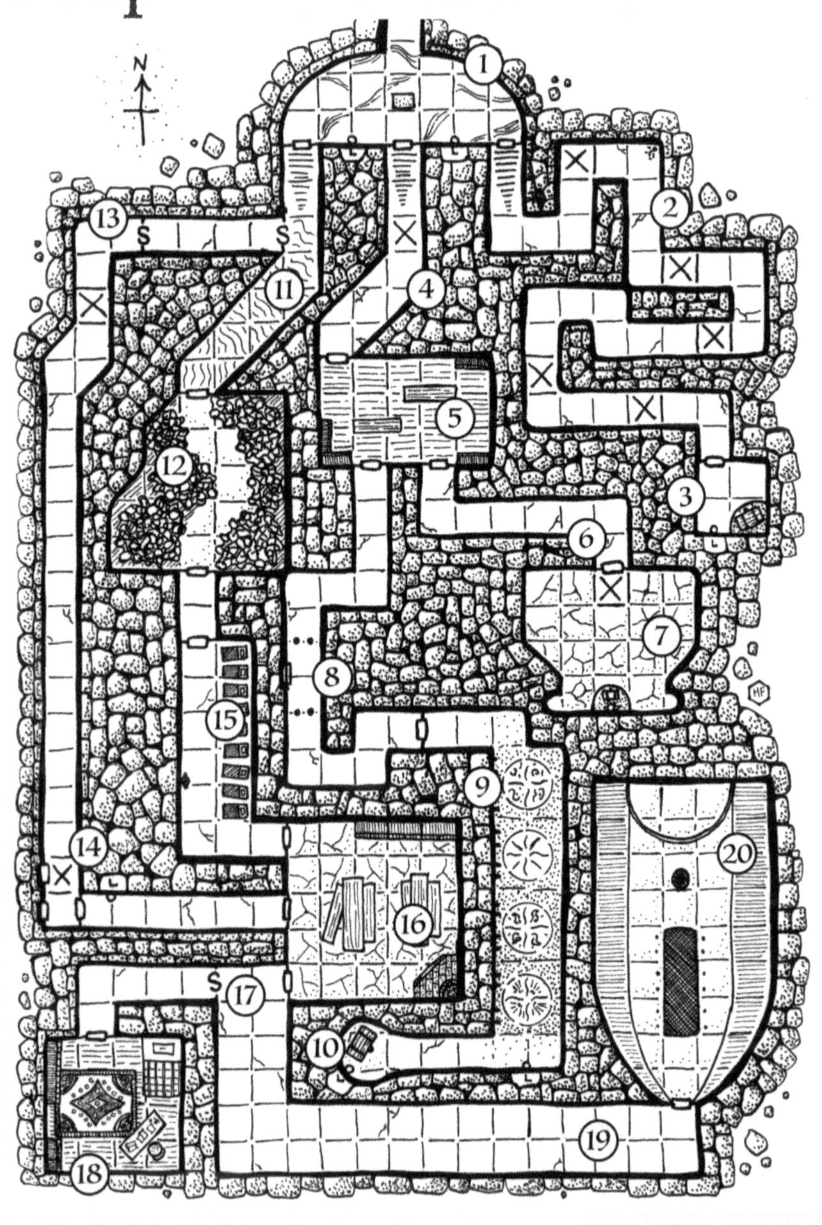

Areas

1 - Entrance

In a flash, you suddenly find yourselves inside a semi-circular room, a ramp behind you leading up to what you figure must be the crypt. From the musty air and the dampness, you can confirm you are underground. Strewn about are a few   stone fragments of what looks like a smashed stone coffin, likely from the crypt behind you, perhaps once covering a secret entrance to where you are now.

Before the light of the magic that brought you fades, you notice a large, raised, stone tablet in the middle of the room, resembling a tombstone. Past it are three stone doors.

The floor tiles are well worn up to the tombstone and then to the western most door.

GM's Notes

Adding light

Shining some light reveals:

- the floor is made of carved dark-grey marble tiles.
- the walls are carved stone.
- Between each of the stone doors is a shiny lever. Each lever consists of a thick metal bar and an ornate copper end that looks like a dragon's skull.

Potential encounters

The party will return to this room at least twice over the course of the adventure. Each time they do, and optionally this first time, they could encounter a group of ogres on their way out or simply checking for unwelcome visitors.

There's a 1-in-6 chance of running into 1d4+2 Blessed Ogres, each armed with a Club +1 and slings, with a pouch of rocks.

Blessed Ogres

AC:5 [14], HD 4+1 (19hp), Att 1x Club (1d10), 1x Sling (1d6+2) THAC0 15 [+4], MV 90' (30'), SV D10 W11 P12 B13 S14 (4), ML 10, AL Lawful Evil, XP: 125, TT C, Abilities: Dark Sight, +1 Save vs Spells

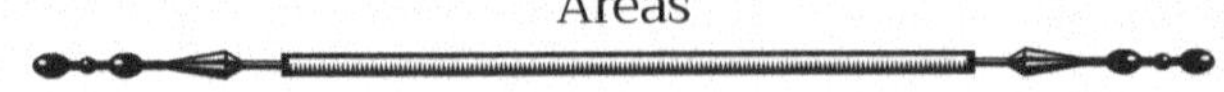

Lever system

There are two fancy-looking levers here:

- Eastern lever. This one is between the middle door and the eastern door in Area 1. This one is able to be moved at the start of the adventure and opens the eastern door. Pulling the lever again closes the eastern door.

- Western lever. This one is between the western and middle door in Area 1. It is locked in position until the lever in Area 3 is pulled. Once unlocked, it will open the middle door. Pulling the lever again closes middle door and, if it is open, the western door.

All three of the doors are made of two-foot-thick stone and have anti-magical powder in them which renders them immune to magical effects.

Tombstone and how the ogres get in and out

The writing on the tombstone is covered in thick dust. Brushing it off reveals a phrase in an old version of common: "Do not disturb Solonark's slumber for it is earned, his treasures deserved."

On the back of the tombstone, near the bottom and hard to see, are two small holes. They have a significant number of scratches around them. By using their crypt keys, Furvik and the ogres are able to unlock the western lever (first hole) and switch the western lever's function (second hole) from opening the middle door to opening the western door. It all resets after 5 minutes with the western door closing. This could allow the party to see ogres leaving into Area 11 but being unable to follow (if you like adding some spice).

As mentioned earlier in *About the Crypt*, the players shouldn't be able to pick the lock successfully or use a crypt key until later in the adventure. However, any failed attempt to pick it will trigger an alarm in Area 15, 16, and 19 which cannot be heard from Area 1.

2 - WINDING AND TRICKY

Passing through the eastern doorway, you see smooth stairs descending in front of you for about twenty feet, then extending in a corridor for another ten feet before turning. It appears to have an elaborate geometric pattern of black and grey tiles.

There's a mildewy breeze flowing past you and the walls feel like they are eating sound.

GM's Notes

Covered crypt poison pit traps

The hidden pit traps are not yet activated. Pulling the lever in Area 3 activates them. Otherwise, the hidden pit traps appear as a normal part of the tiled floor.

Once activated, the poison pit traps are as described earlier in *About the Crypt.* In brief: 1d8 damage, Save vs Poison or -1 to STR, DEX, and WIS, stacking if re-poisoned within 10 minutes). A successful Find Traps reveals the jagged ledge.

Dead body

Ten feet before the door to Area 3 is a dead human in leather armor with puncture wounds and blood stains. It appears to have been there for some time and is facing toward you (away from Area 3). Clutched in their hand is a piece of paper that describes the crypt's entrance with a note at the bottom saying: "Don't get greedy, Charlie."

There's nothing of use on the body. It looks like it's been here about a year.

Door to Area 3

The door appears to be made of wood set in a metal frame. The door is locked and stuck. Opening it requires it to be picked and then bashed or shoved open (total Strength of 20 required).

Unlocking the door disarms a trap within the door itself. If it is shoved or bashed without disarming the trap, spikes jut out causing 1d4 damage. After an hour, the door relocks itself and the trap resets.

3 - Lever and a chest

Finally getting the door open, you see the room has white square tiles. In the opposite corner is an iron chest on a two-foot-high podium of white marble. Beside it is a copper-headed lever similar to the ones you saw at the entrance.

The black and silvery-looking chest has some lettering on it which you can't read from the entryway.

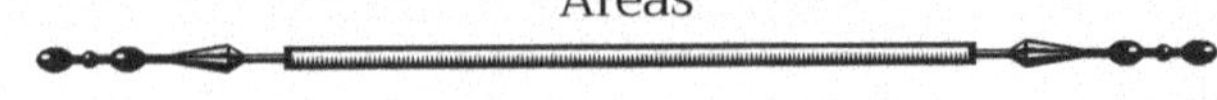

GM's Notes

Door trouble

Once everyone is in the room, the door closes with tremendous force. If someone is in the way, it requires Strength check to hold open or suffer 1d6 damage as it attempts to crush them.

To leave the room requires a total Strength of 30 pushing on the door or doing more than 40hp of damage to the door. The lock only affects trying to open the door from this side.

Lever

The lever looks similar to those at the entrance. It is made of a thick metal bar with an ornate copper end that looks like a dragon's skull when viewed up close.

Pulling the lever gives a satisfying click and it locks into position (see Area 1). Doing this has also activated the covered pit traps in Area 2.

Chest - Trap

The writing on the chest is badly scratched. Anyone with an intelligence of 11 or higher is able to determine that it says: A reward for the greedy and curious.

The chest has no lock and cannot be moved. If the lid is opened, it triggers a dart trap in the room. Darts fire in each direction from the floor, walls, and ceiling every 3 rounds for a total of 5 rounds.

Each time they fire, make each character present Save vs Wands. If they fail, they take 1d4 damage and suffer -1 to AC, dexterity checks, and Save vs Wands for the next 10 minutes. If they get hit again, and fail the save again, the penalty increases (from -1 to -2, from -2 to a maximum of -3) and adds 10 more minutes on to the clock. For example, getting hit a second time 9 minutes in results in a -2 for 11 minutes.

The darts dissolve after an hour.

Chest - Inside

Inside the chest is a single, small, cloudy looking gem worth 50gp and an old priestly robe of no value. The gem is stuck and requires some force to take out.

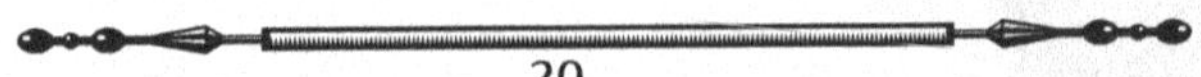

Successfully pulling it out reveals a hole and the false bottom of the chest (allow a thief to notice the false bottom automatically). In the false bottom is a broach wrapped in leather.

The leather has words carefully painted on it and appears old: "for the one in need of protection when the second harm aims to rise from this crypt."

This is a *Broach of Warmth and Grounding* (see *Magic Items*).

4 - SHARP DESCENT

The stone stairs are well-worn and descend sharply for twenty feet after which it levels and proceeds onward for ten feet before jogging to the west.

The slime-covered walls soak in any noise and light, giving you all an uneasy feeling, almost as if the walls were alive.

GM's NOTES

Covered poison pit trap

The poison pit trap at the bottom of the stairs is not active until the door has been opened (see *Trapped Door* below). The poison pit traps are as described earlier in *About the Crypt*. In brief: 1d8 damage, Save vs Poison or -1 to STR, DEX, and WIS, stacking if re-poisoned within 10 minutes). A successful Find Traps reveals the jagged ledge.

This pit re-covers itself when unobserved.

There are two bodies in the pit. One has a magical dagger (+1 to hit, -1 to damage with a minimum of 1 damage) and a Scroll of Light.

Beyond the jog

When the players make it far enough down the corridor they see a door at the end.

The dark wood door is covered in an iron door frame. It's covered in intricate carvings with two words sloppily painted over top: bad books.

The craftsmanship of the carvings is remarkable and looks like it should be part of a royal library rather than being hidden

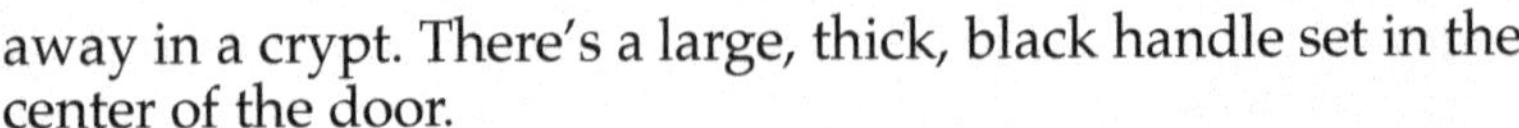

away in a crypt. There's a large, thick, black handle set in the center of the door.

Tales of the door

Any character can make an intelligence or wisdom check on the carvings. A success will reveal that it tells three tales. One is of how greed for knowledge gets the better of the curious. The second tells of how sacrifice is needed and often unexpected. The last seems to be about having patience and that pain, as all things in life, is transient.

Trapped door

Touching the handle results in a shock for 1d8 damage. Holding on to it for a second round results in 1d6 more damage. Holding on to it for a third round results in 1d4 more damage but then, if the player is still alive, the door opens and all damage from the shocks are healed.

A successful Find Traps attempt reveals that the handle is trapped but disarming it is hard (see *Ability Checks and Difficulty*). If disarmed, the damage is 2 points of damage for the first round, 1 for the second, and none on the third. However, the healing mechanism has also been disarmed.

Opening the door activates the poison pit trap at the bottom of the stairs behind the party, making their return a bit more treacherous.

5 - LIBRARY

As you force the door open, you find yourself in what appears to be a lavish library. There's an aroma of old-books and something else, something metallic. Perhaps copper?

Along the walls are small, silver lanterns on hooks shining just enough to give the room character and definition. In the four corners are towering bookcases with a dark brown, lacquered look. They stand fifteen feet high and extend ten feet in both directions. There are four bookcases packed with books of varying sizes and thicknesses.

There are two long tables in the middle of the room. On them are a dozen ink wells organized in perfect rows and columns, a neat pile of quills, and shallow baskets of curled paper.

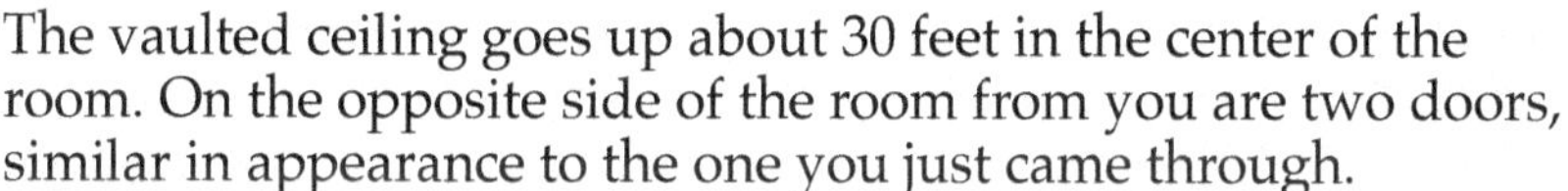

The vaulted ceiling goes up about 30 feet in the center of the room. On the opposite side of the room from you are two doors, similar in appearance to the one you just came through.

There are two wood doors with metal frames to the south. They have a strange symbol on them. The eastern one has words painted on it, but you can't read them from here.

There appears to be no one about, but for some reason, the hairs on the back of your neck are standing up.

GM's Notes

Those aren't bookcases

Three of the four bookcases are a larger, more dangerous, breed of mimic. Though the tables are real, their contents are illusions meant to draw adventurers to the middle of the room. The mimics wait until someone tries to touch one of the books or if the party decides to rest in the room, then one of them attacks.

After a round or two, to determine the strength of the party, either the other two join in or the first one will Feign Death and then all three will chose their moment to attack.

Predatory Mimics

AC 4 [15], HD 10 (50 hp), Att 1x pseudopod 4d4, THAC0 11 [+8], MV 40' (20'), SV D10 W11 P12 B13 S14 (5), ML 10, AL Neutral Evil, XP 1900, Abilities: Intelligent, Sensitive to bright light (-1 to attack & AC), Feign Death, Desperate Charm

Desperate Charm

When there is only one mimic left, and it is down to half its hit points, it screeches loudly and seems to vanish. Emerging from under the table is a badly beaten adventurer, crying with relief at having been freed and wanting to go home. This is actually the predatory mimic.

It claims that a book on the one true bookcase cursed it and for all to stay away.

The fake adventurer asks to be taken out of the crypt and has nothing to offer but its thanks, for now. It claims that its memories are patchy.

There are two likely outcomes:

- *Party accepts the mimic.* If the party escorts the mimic to Area 1, the mimic leaves to plot its revenge for its fallen brethren, perhaps becoming a bed at the local inn. If the party wants the mimic to help them, it pretends to be clumsy and become easily overwhelmed. It will 'accidentally' knock players into traps or if tending to a player on the verge of death, help them along.

- *Party suspicious or attacks.* If the party doesn't accept the mimic, the mimic casts a special charm on them (saves vs spells). Those who are charmed will defend the mimic at all costs for the next one hour and have a positive view of the mimic for the next day. Those who aren't charmed are aware that something is amiss. If forced to fight, the mimic gains 2d6 temporary hit points (for 1 hour) and receives a +1 to hit and damage.

Treasure

Inside the mimics is treasure: 500gp, five gems worth 1000gp each, *Helm of Protection +2*, 4 *Potions of Healing* (1d6+1), *Pin of the Paranoid* (see *Magical Items*) and a strange-looking key with the same symbol on it as on the southern doors for the two southern doors (if it fits the story, the mimic with the key is able to vomit it up).

Real bookcase

One actual bookcase has many moldy and ruined books but if the books are removed, there's an alcove with three additional magical items: *Wand of Fireballs* with 4 charges, *Arm of Naguib* (see *Magical Items*), a *Ring of the Underdog* (see *Magical Items*), and two hands of gold and black marble (one worth 2500gp and the other, clearly nicer, worth 3000gp).

There is one magical book on this bookcase. It has a painted black cover with white chalk eyes drawn on it. If opened, it makes the wielder feel invulnerable to magic but actually gives them a -2 penalty to saving throws versus spells for 1 day.

Northern door

The door is trapped as described in Area 4. Once opened, it will be hard to keep open (requires a strength of 14+).

Southern doors

The two doors to the south are locked with a visible keyhole. The eastern one has sloppy paint on it that reads: "Bad, no go." Attempting to pick the lock and failing results in:

- a shock dealing 1d8 damage for the first time.

- a stronger shock dealing 2d8 the second time

- a series of clicking noises that fill the party with dread (Save vs Spells or suffer from *Fear* as per the spell) for 1d4 rounds.

- Another attempt is treated as a first time.

If the strange key is used (see Treasure above), the trap is deactivated. The trap resets after 10 minutes. There is a keyhole on the other side of the door.

6 - CORRIDOR

The corridor has battered lanterns hung on either side every five feet, ending in a stone door that appears to be half-buried in loose stones, likely carried in from outside.

The door appears to have a scene carefully sculpted into it.

GM's NOTES

Door

The door has a scene carved into it showing an imposing warrior kneeling before the body of a child. There is a tremendous sense of pain and sorrow in the warrior's face and a broken helmet in their hands. Behind the warrior are dozens of little battles between skeletal warriors and other warriors who look identical to the main warrior.

The door has no keyhole or handle; however, there's a smoothed part and indentation hinting that it is to be pushed open.

Lanterns

Upon closer examination, the lanterns look like they have been clawed at and are speckled with what could be dried blood. There is no flame inside them, rather it is some form of light spell that looks like a flame.

If a lantern is removed from the wall, it stops working. If the wielder handles it roughly, like banging it, it drains 1 hp from them (no saving throw) and lights up an area of 20 feet for 10 minutes. It loses its magic if removed from the crypt.

Stuck door and trap

The door resists being opened unless someone with a Strength 12+ gives it a shove. Doing so moves it an inch, making it clear that much more strength is needed to open it any further.

A total of 25 strength or more is needed, which the door still resists until it suddenly springs open, spilling the characters into the covered pit trap. Give the characters a dexterity check to avoid the covered pit, springing over it or out of the way, unaware of it.

7 - SOLONARK'S SORROW

Your eyes are drawn to the twenty-foot tall, majestic statue at the opposite end of the room. The statue is of the same warrior from the carving on the door. He's kneeling, carved to look like he is wearing broken chainmail armor and a cracked helmet, his jeweled eyes twinkling. Before him is a golden chest.

Similar to the library, the ceiling is vaulted. The tiles here are a slick, black marble with white veins. There is the smell of decay in the air, which draws your attention to rotting bodies on the floor in the middle of the room.

The room is only moderately lit, but enough that you can see the side walls are painted. They show a scene of a rolling countryside with burning towns and skeletal warriors battling people from all walks of life. The skeletons are in dark maroon and blue uniforms and are in groups, with a half-skeletal leader, with bright eyes and a flaming sword held aloft, on a hill.

GM's Notes

Covered poison pit trap

As described in Area 6, there is an activated, covered, pit trap. See *About the Crypt* for details. In brief: 1d8 damage, Save vs Poison or -1 to STR, DEX, and WIS, stacking if re-poisoned within 10 minutes). A successful Find Traps reveals the jagged ledge.

Door closes

Once everyone has entered, the door springs back closed. It has a stone handle on the interior. There is a two foot lip between the door and the pit, denoted by white tile. It can be used

safely to get to the door which now can be opened without issue.

Painted scenes on the walls

Within ten feet, characters can see the skeletal warriors are made from actual bone.

Bodies

The bodies in the middle of the room have nothing of value but have been there for several days. They have shoddy leather armor that has been torn to shreds, a broken shield, and shattered swords. Their tunics have the embroidered emblem of the temple that sent the party.

Darkness comes in 2 minutes

After the players have been in the room for 2 minutes, or if they get closer than 10 feet to the side walls or the statues, the Light spell illuminating the room ends and is replaced by a Darkness spell that encompasses the entire room. The statue's eyes twinkle red, giving the statue's face a menacing, skeletal look.

- *Disoriented.* Unless they are near a landmark (the door or the statue) the players become disoriented and have a 3-in-6 chance of walking in a direction other than what they intend because of the darkness.

- *Skeletons in the dark.* As the magical darkness falls over the room, the skeletons silently pull themselves out of the painted wall. There are 10 Solonark Skeletons and two Solonark Skeleton Captains. Once they are all out, they silently attack the players, using chattering teeth to unnerve and misdirect the players. They are magically aware of where the pit is and will not accidentally fall into it.

Solonark's Skeletal Captains

These skeletons still have a piece of their tactical and combat experience, making them particularly deadly. They are dressed in blood-stained armor, wearing leather helms that show their skeleton faces.

The Solonark captains each have two large, jagged-bladed *hand axes +2* (1d8+2 each) and have a *Ring of Solonark's Protection* (+1 vs spells, +2 versus being turned).

AC 2 [18], HD 5 (22 hp), Att 2x by weapon (Enchanted Hand axes +2, 1d8+2), THAC0 15 [+4], MV 80' (40'), SV D10 W11 P12 B13 S14 (4), ML 12, AL Chaotic Evil XP 100, TT None, Abilities:

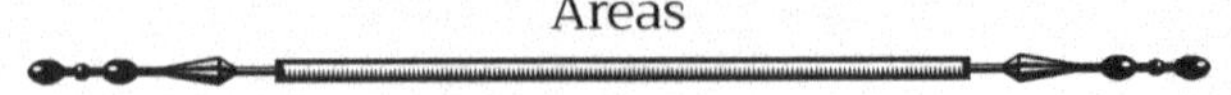

Immunity (Poison, Paralysis, Mind-affecting magic), No scratches (magical weapons only), Silent killer, Shove opponent, Captain

Solonark's Skeletons

These skeletons are dressed in leather armor in Solonark's colors: maroon and blue. They are armed with long swords +1 (1d8+1).

AC 3 [17], HD 3 (15 hp), Att 2x - 1 by weapon (Long sword+1) and 1 by claw (1d4), THAC0 17 [+2], MV 60' (20'), SV D12 W13 P14 B15 S16 (1), ML 12, AL Chaotic Evil, XP 75, TT None, Abilities: Immunity, Barely a scratch (1/2 damage), Silent Killer

After the battle

With the skeletons defeated, the magical darkness lifts and the statue's eyes stop glowing. Subtly, the painted walls start to regenerate bones over the skeletons. After an hour, if the party hasn't left, another of Solonark's Skeletal Captains and 5 Solonark's Skeletons emerge to fight whoever is still there. They won't have magical weapons nor Rings of Solonark's Protection.

Shadows at the back / alcoves

The shadows at the back of the room reveal alcoves, in each of which there is a strange, bubbling fountain.

Drinking from them heals someone 1d8+1, up to twice a day. Any water taken from the room loses its magical effect.

Solonark's Chest

The chest that lays before the statue is made of golden and black metal. It is two feet across, a foot wide, and a foot tall. The chest is locked.

Inside the chest is a *Ring of Regeneration* (+1 hp/round), an *Orb of the Undead* (see *Magical Items*), as well as a child's silver locket. Holding the locket gives a sense of grief and loss. While it has little value (20gp), there's a sense that it's important. If someone receives the *Mark of Solonark* then when wearing the locket, they gain +1 wisdom (maximum of 19).

Solonark's Statue

The statue is remarkably well sculpted, making anyone who looks at it for a while wonder if Solonark was a giant simply turned to stone.

- *Insight.* If anyone studies the statue with an intelligence higher than 12 *and* a wisdom higher than 12, they will feel connected to it and be overcome with a momentary sense of grief at the loss of a son. The scene on the walls now looks different to them, showing terrible people doing horrible things as being the ones attacked by skeletons, skeletons who are the undying forms of noble warriors.

- *Mark of Solonark.* If the statue is left alone (the sword and eyes left alone), the party discovers upon exiting the room they have been given the *Mark of Solonark* as a magical tattoo on their backs. It grants them a permanent +1 to saving throws versus poison and paralysis and the ability to detect skeletons within 60 feet up to 3x per day.

- *Statue's sword.* The statue has a tattoo of a sword on one of its arms that if investigated, turns out to be a real sword covered in stone dust. It is a *Long sword of Solonark.*

- *Jeweled eyes.* Its jeweled eyes are cursed sapphires, each one worth 1000gp but giving whoever possesses them a -1 to AC and a -1 to saving throws. Those with the *Mark of Solonark* find the magic reversed, giving them instead a -1 penalty on saving throws versus poison and paralysis until the eyes are restored.

8 - CORRODED CORRIDOR

This corridor has a strange, sharp odor that bites at your senses. You notice the tiles are stained yellow and there appears to be piles of ash scattered about up to where the corridor bends.

GM NOTES

Around the bend

The players come across a part of the corridor with two, one-foot-wide holes in the ground on the north and two stone beams coming out of the floor to the south of the outline of a door. Between the stone beams are spikes that prevent anyone from passing. The stone beams, door, and floor are covered in yellow dust.

The door and the hands

Rubbing off the thick dust from the door reveals two small handles in the middle, looking like a large bi-fold cupboard

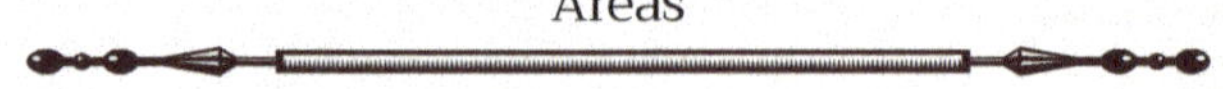

door. Inside is a dust-covered chiseled alcove with two stone hands outstretched.

The left hand is low, at knee height. In it is a small gold and black skull. The right hand is at shoulder height with nothing in it.

Removing the dust from the rest of the alcove reveals the following text: "In pursuit of all things, the value of the desired is always greater than that which is had."

How the puzzle works

The puzzle is a simple weight puzzle. Initially the left hand is higher and the beams to the south are up, blocking passage. By putting more weight in, or hanging from, the right hand (at least ½ pound more), this will cause the left hand to be lower than the right hand and the southern beams will lower into the ground.

Five minutes later, the northern beams will rise out of the floor, blocking passage and requiring that the right hand now be given at least ½ pound more of weight than the left hand has.

How the puzzle's trap works

A successful *Find Traps* attempt will reveal that there's an acid cloud trap that cannot be disarmed but there's a method to how the puzzle and trap works:

- If the weight in the lower hand is reduced, it will trigger the trap.
- If the higher hand is not made the lower hand within 3 rounds of starting, it will trigger the trap.
- If both hands are pushed up or pulled down, it will trigger the trap.

When the trap is triggered, all of Area 8 is filled with a thick green-yellow acid cloud causing 1d6 damage per round and lasts 1d4 rounds before dissipating.

The skull

Inspecting the skull reveals it is remarkably well-made. A rough appraisal would be 2000gp. If jostled side to side, it's clear that's it's heavy, likely about 20 pounds. It is a *Skull of Krossis* (see *Magical Items*).

Brute force

The stone beams can be broken through sheer force, allowing for an escape however they can withstand 50hp of damage. They magically reform in 10 minutes, pieces raising into the air and grafting themselves back in place.

The spikes sticking out of the beams regrow if damaged.

Door at the end of the hall

The door at the end of the hall is stone and has been etched by the acid gas over time. It has a firm stone handle sculpted into it. The door opens slowly, taking 1d4 rounds to get it open. Holding it open takes

Opening the door causes the northern stone beams to come up, preparing the puzzle-trap for the party's return.

9 - Gauntlet of Courage

The door opens and immediately you are hit with a peculiar mixture of the smell of charcoal and rotten eggs, making your eyes gently water.

The walls and ceiling are made of volcanic, porous, pumice-like stone. This stands in strange contrast to the refined workmanship of the decorative tiles. There appear to be four sets of tiles, each a different color and theme.

On the third set of tiles are charred remains and what appears to be metallic slag, potentially the remains of weapons and armor.

At the far end, you can see what appears to be a large, shiny lever with a copper head.

GM's Notes

Door back to Area 8

The entrance door is heavy, with green-yellow dust on the outside and charred black on the inside. After entering, the door quickly adds more and more pressure to close (requiring 15 strength to be held open the first round, then 5 more strength each round until it closes). Once it closes, it locks.

It can only be disarmed by pulling the lever in Area 10.

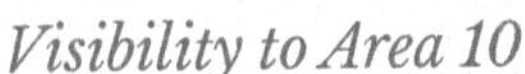

Visibility to Area 10

Only when a character has reached the end of Area 9 will they see the passageway to Area 10.

Deadly corridor

Each set of tiles is covered in decorative symbols and has its own trap. A character with an intelligence, or wisdom, of 13 or greater may make a related ability check to determine if they can figure out what the symbols are indicating.

Anyone stepping on to a tile has a 3-in-6 chance of triggering the trap. Every two rounds, the traps reset. Anyone climbing over a tile is affected by the trap if it is triggered.

First - Anti-Magic dust

Anyone on these tiles must Save vs Breath Weapon or be hit with a dose of anti-magic dust. Failing results in being covered in the dust and the nullification of any magical benefits (or penalties) from magical items, spells, potions, etc. When coated, the individual is unable to cast spells or use scrolls. The effect lasts for 1 hour per dose and cannot be washed off - only time numbs its effect.

The symbols on these tiles make reference to being covered to protect from evil rain. If a character is covered in a blanket, they are immune to the effects of the dust. The blanket, however, will not gain any anti-magical properties.

Second - Weakness darts

A storm of poisoned darts launches from every direction. Save vs Breath Weapon or take 2d4 damage and have a -2 penalty to all saving throws for 1 hour.

The symbols on these tiles make a reference to singing. If the players sing while on these tiles, they receive a +3 bonus to their saving throw from the darts.

Third - Fireball

Liquid fire pours in from the ceiling over the tiles. Take 3d6 damage or Save vs Breath Weapon for half. Note this is not affected by the anti-magic dust.

The symbols on these tiles have been burned away, leaving any hope of knowing how to resist its effects lost to the ages.

Fourth - Hands of life-stealing

Skeletal hands come out of the walls, ceiling, and floor to grab anyone on these tiles. Targets must Save vs Paralysis or be touched and have 1d6 hp of life drained from them per round. Each round they can make another save to try and break free.

The symbols for these final tiles show spilling water about. This is actually holy water, and if put on the tiles, stops the trap from triggering. If put on someone affected, it heals them from the life drain.

Lever

At the end of the corridor is a shiny metal lever about three feet long with a poorly crafted dragon head made of copper.

This is a lever does nothing and is trapped. The real lever is in Area 10. Anyone who touches this lever must Save vs Poison or lose 1d4hp per round for 1d6 rounds.

10 - Broken wall, small room

You notice a dark passage carved into the rock that heads to the west. In the distance, you see something twinkling with the colors of gold and copper.

Chest

The black and gold chest is two-foot-square and a foot tall. It is not locked but it is trapped.

Attempting to open the chest, or failing to disarm the trap, results in all of Area 10 being flooded with a strange, orange gas. All within the passageway must Save vs Poison or be unable to speak (including cast spells) for 1 hour.

Inside the chest is an Amulet of the High Librarian (see *Magical Items*) and a simple looking locket (similar to the one from Area 7). The locket is a Locket of Protection, offering a +1 bonus to AC and Saving Throws vs Breath Weapon when worn.

Underneath the chest

Under the chest is a loose tile with a short sword wrapped in leather. The leather has writing in the same script as the item from Area 3. It reads: "for the one in need of arms when the second harm aims to rise from this crypt."

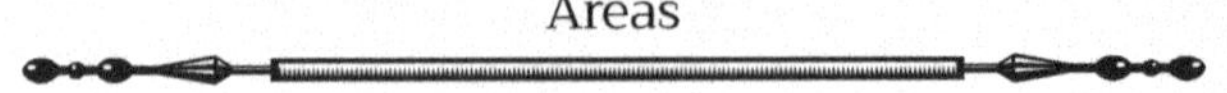

The sword is a Short Sword of the Flame (see *Magical Items*).

Lever

When a player is within 10 feet of the chest, they notice a small lever in the wall. The lever is made of stone and has a well-crafted dragon head made of copper (which cannot come off without destroying the lever).

The lever is in the up position. When pulled downward, it opens the door to in Areas 4, 5, 8, 9 (all the way back to Area 1) and opens the door in Area 1 that leads to Area 11. The doors all close again in 30 minutes.

11 - SLIPPERY STEPS

Standing at the stone doorway, you see a steep descent before you along slimy, worn-smooth steps. There's a putrid smell in the air that turns your stomach. The walls are covered in a thin layer of a dark brown, tacky fluid.

GM's NOTES

Oily liquid

The corridor is leaking a strange, oily liquid from above and into the walls, on the floor, everywhere.

If someone tries to move more quickly than a slow walk, they should make a hard dexterity check (see *Ability Checks and Difficulty*). If they fail, they fall and take 1d4 damage.

Fire hazard

Given that everything is covered in a thin coating of oil, it won't take much to make the entire corridor erupt in flames. For example:

- Someone falls while carrying a torch or lantern.
- Someone uses a flame-based magical item or spell.
- Someone in metal armor and weapons falls (possible spark).

If the area bursts into flame, all characters and characters within take 4d6 damage immediately and 2d6 for the following three rounds until the flame is out.

After the flames have ceased, Area 11 is covered in a thick, choking cloud of smoke for one hour. Anyone moving through

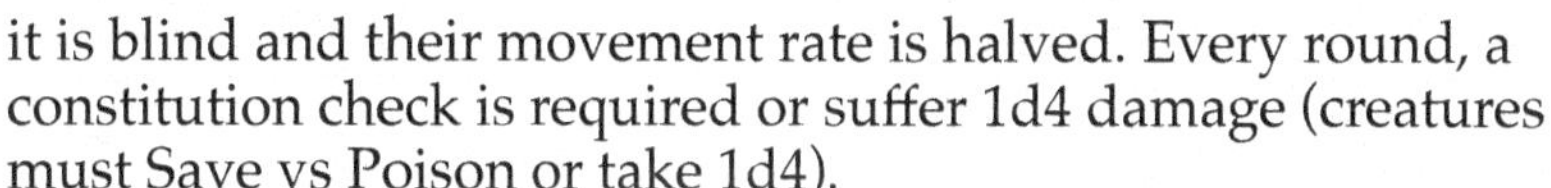

it is blind and their movement rate is halved. Every round, a constitution check is required or suffer 1d4 damage (creatures must Save vs Poison or take 1d4).

The oily residue returns within 1d4 hours, recreating the opportunity for another inferno.

Secret door

Hidden by shadows on the wall next to the secret door lies a tiny keyhole. This provides the only means for opening the secret door. Discovering this keyhole is challenging but offers no hint as to what it is for.

A crypt key is required to unlock it. Any failed attempt to pick the lock gives a 1d8 shock and activates an alarm heard in Areas 15, 16, and 19. Picking the lock is hard (see *Ability Checks and Difficult*).

The secret door leads to what appears to be an unfinished corridor as the walls aren't chiseled smooth toward the end. It actually ends in another secret door.

12 - Carnage Room

Opening this door unleashes a horrible stench upon you that burns the eyes and nose, and you feel an oily film coating your exposed skin. You feel like you are going to vomit violently *(see GM's Notes:Horrific stench below)*.

Before you is a grotesque sight. The bloody remains of humanoid creatures in various states of decomposition are piled up on the right and left, mixed with tin cans, broken shields, swords, and bows, and trash. The pile is over eight feet high with a four-foot-wide path butchered through it.

GM's notes

Southern door

Characters cannot see the far end of this area as the heaps of corpses and garbage block their view after the first fifteen feet.

The door appears to be a standard wooden door and is locked. It can be bashed open or the lock picked. The next door, leading directly to Area 15, is locked and has a simple trap. If

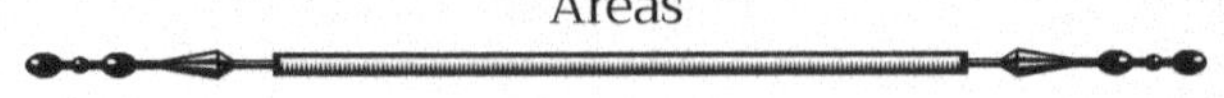

the door is opened, without the trap being disarmed, it triggers an alarm in Area 15 which can be heard by the party.

Horrific stench

When the door opens, everyone within 40 feet of the door must constitution check or be partially impaired (-1 to hit, -1 AC) as they retch for the next 10 minutes.

For every round someone is in Area 12, they must make another constitution check or suffer stacking penalties (-1 becomes -2, -2 becomes -3, to a maximum of -3) and the time accumulates (from 10 minutes to 20, to a maximum of 30 minutes).

Unstable heaps

Disturbing any of the heap has a 1-in-6 chance of causing it to collapse and partially bury a character for 1d4 rounds. If partially buried, they have an AC penalty of -3.

Lurking enemies

There are three semi-intelligent ooze-based creatures, called ozers, lurking and waiting to attack. On either side of the room, hiding in the heaps, is one ozer, with a third clinging to the ceiling.

The ozers will wait until the party is in the middle of the room before attacking, preferring to have surprise. They are able to move through the heaps and trash unimpeded. The ozers won't leave the room if possible.

AC 5 [14], HD 5 (25hp), Att 1x smother (1d8) or 2x pseudopods 1d4, THAC0 13 [+6], MV 10' (3'), SV D10 W11 P12 B13 S14 (4), ML 10, AL Neutral, XP 1,200, NA 1 (0), TT C, Abilities: Surprise, Smother, Climber, Immunity (Poison).

Treasure

Once the ozers are defeated, the heaps are more stable and can be searched. The party can find:

- Four burlap sacks that say flour but actually have 1000gp each
- One sack saying oats but has 250sp
- Half a hay-filled mattress stuffed with 5 gems worth 1000gp each
- A pair of Gloves of Spider Fingers (see *Magical Items*)

- A crypt key (for unlocking secret doors)
- A wooden box with 6 slime-covered Potions of Extraordinary Healing (3d6+3).

13 - SECRET CORRIDOR

A corridor with smooth, chiseled walls, floors, and ceilings, expertly carved so that they resemble large tiles, lies beyond the door. The air here is slightly stale, with a hint of body odor.

The entire passageway is carved from rock with details making it look like the floor and ceiling have tiles. The passageway gradually slopes downward.

At the first corner, your attention is drawn to a keyhole with a golden circlet around it. It's surrounded by hundreds of light scratches in what must be soft stone.

GM's NOTES

Covered poison pit trap

There's an activated, covered poison pit trap. See *About the Crypt* for details. In brief: 1d8 damage, Save vs Poison or -1 to STR, DEX, and WIS, stacking if re-poisoned within 10 minutes). A successful Find Traps reveals the jagged ledge. Five feet before, on the ground, and five feet after the trap is a tiny keyhole.

Using a crypt key in the keyholes deactivates the pit trap for 5 minutes.

Another keyhole

There's another keyhole on the southern side of the pit, again with a golden circlet around it and again surrounded by hundreds of light scratches.

Potential encounter

There's a 2-in-6 chance the party encounters a group of Blessed Ogres (1d4+2) on their way out to get supplies. The ogres know they are supposed to attack anyone they don't recognize.

If the party is able to make the ogres not immediately attack for whatever reason, for example by appearing as ogres, the ogres ask the party for the password. This is a Furvik trick as there is no password. The ogres will pretend the party got the answer

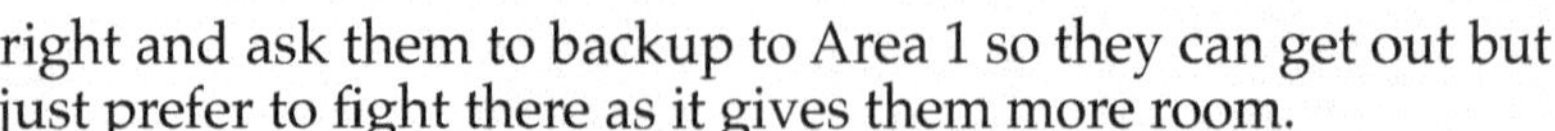

right and ask them to backup to Area 1 so they can get out but just prefer to fight there as it gives them more room.

One of the ogres has a crypt key on them. They are all armed with spiked clubs and slings. Each ogre has 6-8 large rocks in a sack on their belts.

The ogres have trained to fight in narrow spaces allowing them to have one on their knees for melee (penalty of -2 to AC), another standing over them slightly stooped, and a third using a sling from the side.

Blessed Ogres

AC:5 [14], HD 4+1 (19hp), Att 1x Club (1d10), 1x Sling (1d6+2) THAC0 15 [+4], MV 90' (30'), SV D10 W11 P12 B13 S14 (4), ML 10, AL Lawful Evil, XP: 125, TT C, Abilities: Dark Sight, +1 Save vs Spells

14 - TRICKY ENTRANCE

At the end of the corridor, you see what at first looks like two doors on the western side, but it turns out they are large stone panels with a copper handle in the middle of each of them. On the eastern side of the corridor is a stone door with a copper handle as well.

On the floor, at the foot of the two stone panels are a set of symbols etched into the tile. It is a sequence of some kind.

GM's NOTES
Symbols and Puzzle

The symbols give instructions for opening the stone door. There is also a hard-to-find keyhole in the floor in front of the stone door for a crypt key.

The symbols are similar to those found in Area 8. If the players were successful in deciphering the symbols, or if they had received the rumor about the symbols, give them a +2 bonus on the intelligence Check to figure out the symbols.

The correct sequence is:

- Pull handle of northern panel
- Push southern panel without touching handle
- Push northern panel without touching handle

- Pull handle of southern panel

Getting each correct step in the sequence gives a satisfying click sound. Getting the sequence wrong causes the covered poison pit trap to open for one minute before closing again.

The poison pit trap is as described earlier in *About the Crypt*. In brief: 1d8 damage, Save vs Poison or -1 to STR, DEX, and WIS, stacking if re-poisoned within 10 minutes). A successful Find Traps reveals the jagged ledge.

Past the stone door, on the way to Area 16

Beyond the stone door, on the way to Area 16, is a lever. Pulling this lever opens the stone door to Area 16.

The door to Area 16 is made of paneled wood badly nailed together and hanging askew. It has clearly been beaten up and repaired many times over. There's an oddly inviting smell coming from beyond the door, along with light.

15 - Barracks

Opening the door, you are met with a smokey haze and the pungent odor of unwashed bodies, urine, and feces.

Lined up along the eastern wall are beds of blankets atop hay and various small items, likely personal belongings, atop wooden crates.

Sitting on a chair, by a hole in the ground, along the western wall is a sloppily painted sign that reads: "Pees and poops."

Beside the northern door is a key on a hook and a large barrel with a human-like forearm and hand sticking out of it.

GM's notes

Occupants and alarms

If the alarm was sounded, then there are six ogres here waiting for someone to enter:

- two guarding the northern door with clubs ready
- two guarding the southern door with clubs ready
- two in the middle of the room with their slings ready

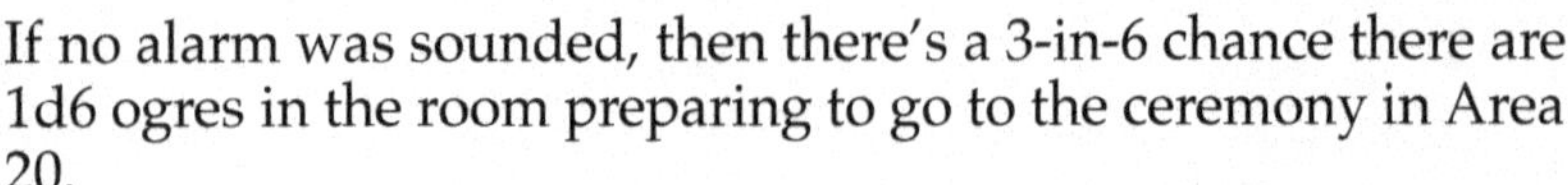

If no alarm was sounded, then there's a 3-in-6 chance there are 1d6 ogres in the room preparing to go to the ceremony in Area 20.

They are wielding clubs +1 and a sling with a pouch of rocks.

Blessed Ogres

AC:5 [14], HD 4+1 (19hp), Att 1x club (1d10), 1x Sling (1d8+2), THAC0 15 [+4], MV 90' (30'), SV D10 W11 P12 B13 S14 (4), ML 10, AL Lawful Evil, XP: 125, TT C, Abilities: Dark Sight, +1 Save vs Spells

Treasure

The key on the hook by the northern door is a crypt key. Among the ogre belongings are:

- a small sack of 100sp

- a deck of large normal cards

- the head of a halfling

- a strange coin in a box with the clumsily scrawled words: "Bad no good coin." It's a Coin of Devouring (see *Magical Items*).

- A piece of stiff chain 18" long. This is a Wand of Chains (see *Magical Items*).

About the ozers

The ogres use Area 12 as a dumping ground for bodies, food refuse, and all manner of garbage. They are aware of the ozers, who are happy to be regularly fed by the ogres.

16 - Kitchen

The first thing that strikes you about this room is that it smells strangely wonderful and inviting, like home cooking after a trek through the rain.

There's a fireplace in the south-eastern corner with a small cauldron of something bubbling away, two large tables with chairs, and cabinets along the northern wall with wooden bowls, mugs, and spoons.

As inviting as the room is, it is, however, occupied.

GM's Notes

Occupants

If any alarms have been sounded there will be 1d6+3 ogres in the room, with weapons ready. They will each have 3 large, nasty spears with them for throwing (1d10 damage), in addition to their club and sling. They will immediately flip over the tables for cover (+2 to AC or as stated in your system).

If no alarm was sounded, there are 1d4+1 ogres here making food or eating, their clubs and slings on the table.

Blessed Ogres

AC:5 [14], HD 4+1 (19hp), Att 1x Club (1d10), 1x Sling (1d6+2) THAC0 15 [+4], MV 90' (30'), SV D10 W11 P12 B13 S14 (4), ML 10, AL Lawful Evil, XP: 125, TT C, Abilities: Dark Sight, +1 Save vs Spells

Chance encounter with Kokeen

There's a 2-in-6 chance the high priest Kokeen is in the room. She is immediately recognizable as a high-priest with her long blue and purple robes, necklaces, and tattooed, bald head. Any divine-type characters (Clerics, Paladins, etc.) will sense power and calm from her.

Kokeen is not eager to fight the party, rather to know why they are there and to get them to leave. If the party shares the story about the murdered family member, Kokeen will be genuinely surprised and feel that it isn't right. She will take it as a sign that Furvik has been lying and then takes the ogres present and leaves the crypt.

If the party tries to attack her, she fights for 2 rounds before breaking off and heading to Area 20 to be part of the ceremony.

AC: 5 [14], HD 4+2 (22hp), Att 1 x Mace (1d12), THAC0 15 [+4], MV 90' (30') SV D10, W11 P12 B13 S14 (4), ML 10, AL Lawful Evil, XP 150, Abilities: Spells, Blessed against Spells (+2 on Saves vs Spells), wields a Mace of Plant Disruption (+2 to hit and damage, immune to entanglement and plant-related spells)

Treasure

There are 20 plates, mugs, and utensils worth 10gp altogether.

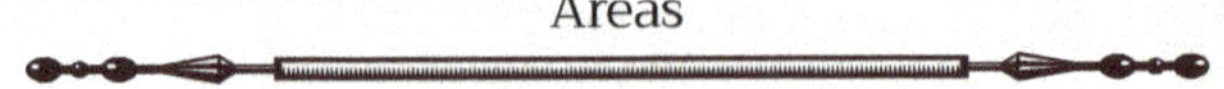

17 - Secret Door to Leader's chambers

As the door opens, you are met with cool air and dampness. With each step, you feel the temperature slowly dropping.

You notice the painted walls and floor once were covered in an epic scene which has recently had sections scratched off and other parts painted over, ruining it. The floor is carved to look like tiles, but likely are sheer rock. The ceiling has intriguing symbols but not discernible pattern.

On the wall opposite you is a gold circlet embedded in the stone. There is a significant amount of dried blood below it.

GM's Notes

Circlet

In the middle of the circlet is a small keyhole which unlocks and opens the secret door. The lock can be picked but it takes ten minutes, allowing for another Potential Encounter (see below). Alternatively, a crypt key can be used.

Connecting corridor

The corridor behind the secret door, which leads to the Leader's Chambers, has a blood stain on the other side of the secret door as if someone had opened it and then been killed.

The door to Furvik's Chambers is covered in stone with a large red lacquer circle and with a small gold circlet and a black stone handle in that. The door is slightly ajar.

Potential encounter

Every ten minutes, there's a 2-in-6 chance there are 1d4+2 ogres on their way out from Area 20 and heading out of the crypt. They are armed with large, nasty spears +1 and attack anyone they don't recognize, as well as sound the alarm.

If they get to sound the alarm, a 1d6+2 more Blessed Ogres arrive from Area 20.

Blessed Ogres

AC:5 [14], HD 4+1 (19hp), Att 1x Spear (1d12), THAC0 15 [+4], MV 90' (30'), SV D10 W11 P12 B13 S14 (4), ML 10, AL Lawful Evil, XP: 125, TT C, Abilities: Dark Sight, +1 Save vs Spells

18 - Furvik's Chambers

As soon as you open the door, a softly glowing orb rises from a thin porcelain pedestal in the far corner of the room behind a desk and chair. As the orb brightens, it illuminates the room revealing the vaulted ceiling, outlining the bed in the north eastern corner, and drawing the large wall-to-wall bookcase on the western wall from the shadows.

The floor is partially covered by what was once a rug of remarkable taste and privilege, but now is dirty, frayed, and worn thin.

GM's Notes

Orb

The orb is an *Orb of Light* (see *Magical Items*). If covered by a cloth, like the one in the desk, it gently lowers to the ground and stops glowing. It can be reactivated with a thought.

Ozers

There are two ozers hiding in the shadows of the ceiling. They are trained and kept by the leader, Furvik. They know what he and his ogres smell like, so they will be waiting for an opportunity to drop on the party and attack.

AC 5 [14], HD 5 (25hp), Att 1x smother (1d8) or 2x pseudopods 1d4, THAC0 13 [+6], MV 10' (3'), SV D10 W11 P12 B13 S14 (4), ML 10, AL Neutral, XP 1,200, NA 1 (0), TT C, Abilities: Surprise, Smother, Climber, Immunity (Poison).

Bookcase

The bookcase looks exactly like the mimic-bookcases from Area 5 but isn't.It is sparsely covered in books that have been knocked about, with a pile on the floor of ones that have been ripped apart and burned.

The books:

- there are five well-worn novels set in a fairy-tale land with airships and windup technology (10sp each)
- one about levers, pulleys, and the wonders of technology (20sp)
- a thin book of a few dozen pages with singed edges. It's written in a theocratic script. Divine-type characters (Clerics, Paladins, etc.) characters can read it. It tells of those who will come to stop the rise

of a mad goblin and spirit; how items were placed in the final home of Solonark; and wishing those heroes well. It has names of everyone in the party.

Hidden behind a loose panel in the bookcase is an intriguing looking tome. It's a *Tome of the Charming Smile* (see *Magical Items*).

Storage box

The dresser has goblin-sized clothing in it including folded silk robes, undergarments, and sandals. Hidden among the clothes is a *dagger +2* and two *Potions of Healing* (1d6+1).

At the back of one of the boxes is a blade trap which delivers 1d4 damage.

Desk

In the south-eastern corner is a writing desk with a chair. It is covered in inkwells, rolls of scroll paper, a small basket of quills, and a cloth of some kind. There's a plate and mug, reinforcing the idea that someone's been there recently.

The rolls of scroll paper are notes and correspondence. The legible ones are from an apparent mole in the temple with updates over many months as to relics and the transportation of the gauntlets, with lots of pleading for mercy and asking to stop making them spy on the elder's activities. They ask that they please leave [family member] alone, they are innocent in all of this.

Hidden in the drawers are:

- *Scroll of Web*
- 2 *Potions of Growth* (increases size and strength, doubling melee damage for 1d6 rounds).

Bed

The bed is very comfortable. Stashed under the mattress is a journal. The journal is hard to make out but shows that Furvik believes the voice he's hearing is of an old god seeking to give him power and that he expects it to consume the life of all the ogres to do it. It is written in a relatively neat handwriting the same as one of the styles used in the notes on the desk.

Under the rug

Hidden beneath the rug is a secret door and tunnel which exits into the cemetery, allowing someone to escape.

Unexpected visitor - Kokeen

There's a 3-in-6 chance that if the players didn't encounter Kokeen in the kitchen (Area 16) that Kokeen walks in on them. She is recognizable as a high-priest and as having a sense of power and calm about her.

She is dressed in long blue and purple priestly robes, necklaces made of rocks and pieces of bark, and has a tattooed, bald head.

Kokeen asks the party what they are doing and what they want. She is troubled that since the ritual started (in Area 20) she cannot hear her god. She feels something is very wrong.

There are two likely paths the party chooses:

- Friendly. She tells the party that Furvik has nearly completed the ritual and give them a scroll which will draw out the time needed to complete it (lengthens it by 3 rounds). She then leaves the crypt feeling she has failed her flock and requires introspection and to reconsider her future.

- **Hostile.** If the party attacks her, she defends herself and attempts to get back to Area 20 to complete the ceremony, convinced now that Furvik was right. Along the way, she intentionally triggers a silent alarm, calling in ogres to Area 19 to lend aid.

AC: 5 [14], HD 4+2 (22hp), Att 1 x Mace (1d12), THAC0 15 [+4], MV 90' (30') SV D10, W11 P12 B13 S14 (4), ML 10, AL Lawful Evil, XP 150, Abilities: Spells, Blessed against Spells (+2 on Saves vs Spells), wields a Mace of Plant Disruption (+2 to hit and damage, immune to entanglement and plant-related spells)

19 - Path to the Temple Door

Turning the corner, the air goes from cool to frosty. There's a sheen of ice coating the floor, ceiling, and walls that thickens as the hallway proceeds toward the large stone door in the northern wall at the end. The sounds of chanting can be heard faintly.

GM's Notes

Alarms and ogres

If any alarms were set off by the party, there are six Blessed Ogres waiting for intruders ready to immediately attack. They are armed with large, nasty spears and slings.

AC:5 [14], HD 4+1 (19hp), Att 1x Spear (1d12), 1x Sling (1d6+2) THAC0 15 [+4], MV 90' (30'), SV D10 W11 P12 B13 S14 (4), ML 10, AL Lawful Evil, XP: 125, TT C, Abilities: Dark Sight, +1 Save vs Spells

Approaching the door

As the party approaches the door, the sound of chanting gets stronger and the hair on the back of their arms and neck stand up.

Any divine-type characters sense a strong, unnatural presence nearby.

Door

The stone door is covered in carvings made hard to see by the ice build-up. The door is able to be pushed open without much effort.

20 - The Crypt's Inner Chamber

Slowly the door gives way, revealing an hazy, icy, and shadowy cavernous chamber with a large statue at the far end. The statue has its arms outstretched toward the sky and its eyes looking down where the figure with the gauntlets are. Its eyes are shimmering with blue-green magical energy.

At its feet, on an elevated white stone platform, is a goblin in strange thin-chain robes wearing oversized, glowing gauntlets - Furvik. His arms are raised high in the air, and he is chanting loudly. There are four large, armed and armored, ogres protecting him.

Lined along the walls are a dozen ogres chanting in a monotone, their eyes shining the same blue-green as the statue and the glow of the gauntlets. They are holding spears that have been decorated with red and black ribbons.

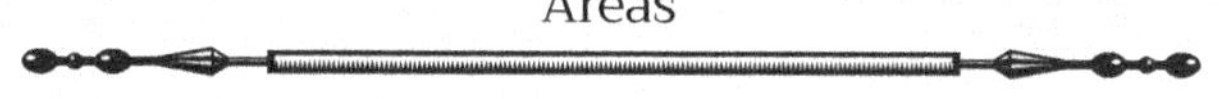

Between the door and the statue is a large brazier, burning incense and producing a smokey haze.

The floor is covered in ice and there are large, javelin-like icicles hang from the 50' high ceiling.

The chanting is reaching a fevered pitch and there is a sense of tremendous evil.

GM's Notes

Kokeen

If the players did not encounter Kokeen in Area 16 or Area 18, or if she returned to the ceremony, she will be standing beside Furvik. She is dressed in long blue and purple priestly robes, necklaces made of rocks and pieces of bark, and has a tattooed, bald head. Her eyes are glowing like the wall ogres.

Large pit

Near the middle of the room is a 10' by 30' open poison spike pit (standard crypt poison pit, see *About the Crypt*: 1d8 and Save vs Poison or suffer -1 STR, DEX, WIS for 10 minutes).

There are several dead bodies in it, some old and some recent additions. There is no safe way to get into the pit and out again, without someone else providing a rope and concentrating on helping for 1-2 rounds.

In the pit is a set of small *Plate Mail +1* and a backpack with 3 *Potions of Extraordinary Healing* (3d6+3).

Slippery floor

The floor is slippery for players who move more than 20' per round - requiring a dexterity check with a -1 penalty per additional 10' they try to move in a given round. Note that if they have a magical item or spell effect that gives them sure footing, no check is needed. If they fail the dexterity check, they are knocked prone and must spend a round getting back up.

What's going on

Furvik is three rounds away from successfully releasing the power in the *Gauntlets of the Ice Demon Kofnar*. He must concentrate, unable to take other actions, for three rounds

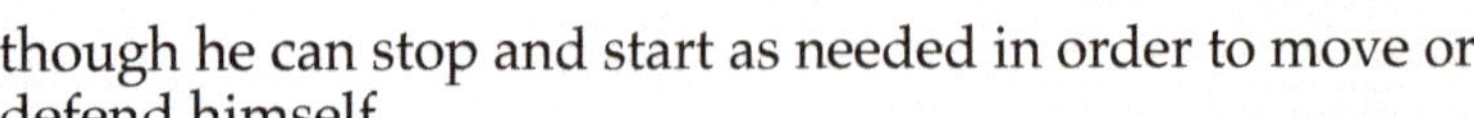

though he can stop and start as needed in order to move or defend himself.

If the party received, and use, the scroll from Kokeen (see Area 18),Furvik requires an additional three rounds of concentration to complete the ritual.

As the ritual completes, the party notices a larger form outlining Furvik, this is the evil spirit. It is unable to be attacked until the ritual is completed when it bonds with Furvik.

Upon completion, Furvik absorbs life from all the living ogres in the room, including Kokeen. This changes them into undead ogres (half their remaining hit points, Kokeen cannot cast spells, no other benefits). Furvik is visibly transformed, becoming large, stronger, taller, his eyes glowing (see the Furvik - Transformed entry below).

Entering quietly

If the party enters quietly, they will be not be noticed until one of the following happens:

- *Noisy.* If they make noise, fall, or cause any form of disruption of the ceremony there's a 3-in-6 chance they are noticed and 1d6+1 of the ogres awaken and attack.

- *Attacks.* Normal attacks cause everyone to become aware, but sneak attacks by a thief or rogue-type against one of the wall ogres will only have a 3-in-6 chance of being noticed. Even a sneak attack against Furvik, or one of the guardian ogres with him, causes everyone to become aware of the party.

- *Close enough.* The players reach the brazier (black circle on the map). Then everyone becomes aware of the party. The ogres only move 20' per round because of the icy floor.

Javelin icicles

The icicles are secure until fighting starts. Then, at the GM's discretion (or 1-in-6 per round) a large icicle falls from the ceiling.

It's recommended to use this for cinematic purposes, like coming between player and opponent, causing a distraction, etc., thereby increasing the tension.

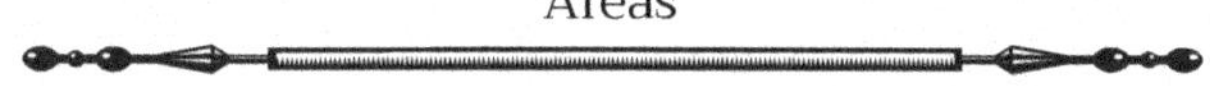

Opponents

12 Wall Ogres

These ogres are standard Blessed Ogres each armed with a spear +1.

AC:5 [14], HD 4+1 (19hp), Att 1x Spear (1d10) THAC0 15 [+4], MV 90' (30'), SV D10 W11 P12 B13 S14 (4), ML 10, AL Lawful Evil, XP: 125, TT C, Abilities: Dark Sight, Blessed against magic (+1 Save vs Spells)

Kokeen

AC: 5 [14], HD 4+2 (22hp), Att 1 x Mace (1d12), THAC0 15 [+4], MV 90' (30') SV D10, W11 P12 B13 S14 (4), ML 10, AL Lawful Evil, XP 150

- **Spells.** Cure/Cause Serious Wounds x2 (2d6+2), Push x2 (Save vs Spells or be thrown back up to 20 feet), Powerful Bless (+2 to AC and to Hit for up to four ogres within 30')
- **Blessed against spells.** The priest has +2 to their Saving Throw against Spells.
- **Well armed.** Has a Mace of Plant Disruption (+2 to hit and damage, double damage against plants and plant-based creatures, immune to entanglement and plant-related spells)
- **Healing.** Kokeen has two Potions of Extraordinary Healing (2d8+1).

Four guardian ogres

These four ogres are on the raised platform with Furvik and are his bodyguards. They won't allow themselves to be drawn more than twenty feet away from him. They are wearing a form of plate armor. They are wielding extra *large sabers +2* (medium-sized creatures must use two hands to wield it).

AC:3 [16], HD 4+1 (25hp), Att 1x Saber (1d12), THAC0 14 [+5], MV 90' (30'), SV D10 W11 P12 B13 S14 (4), ML 10, AL Lawful Evil, XP: 150, TT C

Furvik - before ritual ends

Furvik will stop the ritual and defend himself if needed. Note that he is unaffected by the icy floors.

AC 5 [14], HD 3 (20hp), Att 1x Spell or Gauntlets of the Ice Demon Kofnar (see Magical Items), THAC0 15 [+4], MV 90' (30') SV D11 W12 P11 B11 S12 (M7), ML 10, AL Chaotic Evil, XP 1500

- Amulet of Missile Deflection (+3 AC from magical and normal ranged weapons)
- Gauntlets of the Ice Demon Kofnar (see *Magical Items*)
- Robe of Chains (same AC as chainmail)
- Poisoned Dagger +1 (Save vs Poison or take additional 1d4 damage)
- 1 Potion of Extraordinary Healing (2d8+1)
- 50gp

Furvik's readied spells

- 1st level - Charm Person, Darkness, Magic Missile
- 2nd level - Invisibility, Levitate, Web
- 3rd level - Fireball, Hold Person, Lightning Bolt
- 4th level - Dimension Door

Furvik - transformed

When Furvik transforms, he grows to the size of an ogre. Whereas he was quiet before, now he is interested in taunting and verbally beating the party down, reveling in his new power.

The transformation causes him to:

- Add 40hp
- Gain an option of two icy clawed attacks, the gauntlets now fused to him. These are +3 to hit and do 2d8 damage each.
- Gain a +2 on saving throws versus spells and wands.

Defeating Furvik

If Furvik is killed after having transformed, the gauntlets separate from his body but are spent, no longer having any power.

If he is killed before he is able to transform, the gauntlets are intact but anyone putting them on will find their mind corrupted by the Evil Spirit. Unless the gauntlets are removed within an hour, the player becomes an NPC now seeking to find a place from which to conduct the ritual themselves. The Evil Spirit will be with them, awaiting the opportunity to take over their body fully.

Treasure

The only other treasure hidden in the room is in the brazier itself. There are three gems worth 2000gp each.

The End

The party leaves the crypt and finds an emissary from the temple waiting for them. The party is escorted to the temple where the Elder gives them their reward of 20,000gp for the gauntlets and thanks them for their heroics.

The elder also gives the party a simple, silver ring with the word "Giver" which belonged to [Family Member]. "A reward they'd earned for their wonderful aid to the people of the town."

Potential Connection

The elder could also give the party a handwritten note from the family member, tying to whatever you have planned next.

Creatures

BLESSED OGRES

Furvik's ogre followers have had their abilities boosted by the Evil Spirit. They are usually armed with a club and a sling. They have several large rocks in a pouch.

AC:5 [14], HD 4+1 (19hp), Att 1x Club (1d10), 1x Sling (1d6+2) THAC0 15 [+4], MV 90' (30'), SV D10 W11 P12 B13 S14 (4), ML 10, AL Lawful Evil, XP: 125, NA 2-6, TT C

- **Dark sight.** The ogres have the ability to see in complete and magical darkness. They can see normally but also can see the halo of real and magical light.

- **Blessed against magic.** They have a +1 to their Saving Throws against Spells.

KOKEEN THE OGRE HIGH PRIEST

Kokeen is dressed in long blue and purple priestly robes, necklaces made of rocks and pieces of bark, and has a tattooed, bald head.

AC: 5 [14], HD 4+2 (22hp), Att 1 x Mace (1d12), THAC0 15 [+4], MV 90' (30') SV D10, W11 P12 B13 S14 (4), ML 10, AL Lawful Evil, XP 150

- **Spells.** Cure/Cause Serious Wounds x2 (2d6+2), Push x2 (Save vs Spells or be thrown back up to 20 feet), Powerful Bless (+2 to AC and to Hit for up to four ogres within 30')

- **Blessed against spells.** The priest has +2 to their Saving Throw against Spells.

- **Well armed.** Has a Mace of Plant Disruption (+2 to hit and damage, double damage against plants and plant-based creatures, immune to entanglement and plant-related spells)

PREDATORY MIMICS

These mimics are particularly intelligent, sneaky, and tough. They prefer to work in small groups. Often, they will have one of them attack to determine the strengths and weaknesses of their opponents and quickly feign death. Then all the mimics will attack at a moment of their choosing - gaining surprise.

AC 4 [15], HD 10 (50 hp), Att 1x pseudopod 4d4, THAC0 11 [+8], MV 40' (20'), SV D10 W11 P12 B13 S14 (5), ML 10, AL Neutral Evil, XP 1900, NA 1-4, TT None

- *Intelligent*. They are able to speak the language of anyone they have come into contact with for a day. They can sometimes claim to be gods, to be testing characters, but ultimately want to simply get the upper hand and devour their prey.

- *Sensitive to light*. They are sensitive to bright light (-1 penalty to attack rolls and -1 to AC).

- *Feign death*. They can turn to stone for up to 4 rounds, becoming immune to normal damage. While stone they are unable to move, communicate, or take any action. They do this to feign death and will often take on an exaggerated pose. They are also able to remain perfectly still for long periods of time.

- *Desperate charm*. If the rest of its hunting pack are dead, and the mimic is down to half or less of its hit points, it transforms into a sympathetic form (like a wounded adventurer) and attempts to charm the party (Save vs Spells). If successful, it will get the party to lead it to safety, betraying them if there's a good opportunity or simply leaving otherwise.

Ozer

These are semi-intelligent ooze that are able to form pseudopods to bludgeon opponents or will drop on them to attempt to smother them. They are able to move across gaps up to 10' wide and climb surfaces, though they do so slowly.

AC 5 [14], HD 5 (25hp), Att 1x smother (1d8) or 2x pseudopods 1d4, THAC0 13 [+6], MV 10' (3'), SV D10 W11 P12 B13 S14 (4), ML 10, AL Neutral, XP 1,200, NA 1 (0), TT C

- *Surprise*. It can camouflage itself, looking like any ceiling or floor. Surprise opponents on a 1–4.

- *Smother*. A target who is being smothered is unable to defend itself or attack. Someone else must do damage to the Ozer to get it to release its target. It automatically hits any target it is smothering each round.

- *Climber*. It can climb surfaces.

- *Immunity*. They are immune to poison.

Solonark's Skeletons

These legendary skeletons are significantly stronger and more capable than standard skeletons. They are dressed in soldier's leather armor with the kingdom of Solonark's colors. It is said

they were once mighty warriors who were corrupted by the allure of destroying their enemy at all costs.

AC 3 [17], HD 3 (15 hp), Att 2x - 1 by weapon (Long sword+1) and 1 by claw (1d4), THAC0 17 [+2], MV 60' (20'), SV D12 W13 P14 B15 S16 (1), ML 12, AL Chaotic Evil, XP 75, NA 2-12, TT None

- Immunity. They are immune to poison, paralysis, mind-affecting, and mind-reading magic.
- Barely a scratch. They take half-damage from non-magical bladed weapons such as swords, arrows, axes, and daggers.
- Silent Killer. They move silently, usually until they attack when they chatter. However, they can also decide to use the teeth chattering to draw an opponent toward them or create confusion.

SOLONARK'S SKELETON CAPTAIN

These skeletons still have a piece of their tactical and combat experience, making them particularly deadly. They are dressed in blood-stained armor, wearing leather helms that show their skeleton face. In each hand, they have an axe.

AC 2 [18], HD 5 (22 hp), Att 2x by weapon (Enchanted Hand axes +2, 1d6+2), THAC0 15 [+4], MV 80' (40'), SV D10 W11 P12 B13 S14 (4), ML 12, AL Chaotic Evil XP 100, NA 1-3, TT None

- *Immunity.* They are immune to poison, paralysis, mind-affecting and mind-reading magic
- *No scratches.* No damage from non-magical bladed weapons (swords, arrows, daggers, etc).
- *Silent killer.* They move silently, usually until they attack when they chatter. However, they can also decide to use the teeth chattering to draw an opponent toward them or create confusion.
- *Shove opponent.* If both hand axes hit an opponent, the captain is able to shove the opponent up to 10 feet in a direction of their choice.
- *Captain.* These skeletons are able to coordinate up to 6 other skeletons to perform tactical maneuvers such as flanking opponents, forcing opponents back, etc.

Magical Items

Here you will find the details for all the new magical items you won't find in your system's rulebooks. These have been drawn from various volumes of *Wondrous & Perilous*™ Treasures or perhaps will be in a future one.

<table>
<tr><td colspan="2" style="background:#4a6b2f;color:white">Item Name</td></tr>
<tr><td colspan="2">Allowed Groups/Classes - Power Level</td></tr>
<tr><td colspan="2">Description of the item and summary of its abilities</td></tr>
</table>

LAYOUT AND LEGEND

Each item is laid out in the same style, shown here:

ALLOWED GROUPS/CLASSES

This describes which particular classes are allowed, or not

Name	Classes & Races
Divine	*CLERIC, DRUID, PALADIN, RANGER, BARD*
Magical	*ILLUSIONIST, MAGIC-USER, DROW, DUERGAR, ELF, GNOME, HALF-ELF*
Rogue	*ACROBAT, ASSASSIN, BARD, THIEF, HALFLING, HALF-ORC*
Warrior	*FIGHTER, KNIGHT, PALADIN, RANGER, DWARF, ELF, HALF-ELF, HALF-ORC, SVIRFNEBLIN*

allowed, to use the item. Classes are grouped together in the chart below into four basic categories: Divine, Magical, Rogue, Warrior. There is also a group called Spellcaster. Some classes, and race-as-classes, can exist in more than one group.

The *Divine* group covers the group of classes (and applicable race-as-class) where the character gains abilities, and/or spells, from a god, deity, demon, nature, or something else considered extraordinarily powerful. This covers clerics, paladins, druids, some versions of the bard, as well as most versions of the warlock class that have been back-ported to Old-School systems.

The *Magical* group covers those who have abilities and/or spells, from a magical source like magic-users, illusionists, gnomes and elves (race-as-class).

Spellcasters is the subset of Magical and Divine who actually can cast spells such as Clerics, Druids, Illusionists, Magic-Users, Elf-as-class. Depending on the system you are using, Bards and other classes may be included. Note that if the class will allow spell casting at a higher level than the character currently is, then they do not count as a spellcaster for this purpose.

The previous table groups the classes and race-classes from the *Old-School Essentials*.

POWER LEVEL

This provides an idea of how powerful the item is from: low to medium to high. Some magical items are cursed, or have twists to them, which is included in the calculation for its overall rating.

EXPERIENCE POINTS AND VALUE OF ITEMS

Depending on the system you are using, players may be awarded experience points depending on how powerful and rare a magical item is. Similarly, you may want a suggested gold piece value for each item. See the chart below.

Power Level	Item type	XP	GP
Low	Potion, Elixirs, Tonics	150	400
	Wands, Staves, Rods	600	3,000
	Rings	800	4,000
	Armor, Garments	300	4,000
	Weapons	800	6,000
	Other & Miscellaneous	400	2,500
Medium	Potion, Elixirs, Tonics	250	900
	Wands, Staves, Rods	1200	8,000
	Rings	1200	9,000
	Armor, Garments	1200	7,000
	Weapons	1400	12,000
	Other & Miscellaneous	800	6,000
High	Potion, Elixirs, Tonics	400	2,000
	Wands, Staves, Rods	2000	20,000
	Rings	1800	15,000
	Armor, Garments	2500	15,000
	Weapons	3500	30,000
	Other & Miscellaneous	2500	25,000
Legendary	Potion, Elixirs, Tonics	750	5,000
	Wands, Staves, Rods	3000	40,000
	Rings	2500	30,000
	Armor, Garments	5000	60,000
	Weapons	7000	90,000
	Other & Miscellaneous	3500	40,000

Items

Amulet of the High Librarian

Spellcaster– Medium

This large amulet glows in the presence of spellbooks, scrolls, and magical runes.

- **Spell taker**. You are able to copy spells from other spellbooks into your own. You can also copy scrolls into your spellbook without failing.

- **Spell stealer**. You can use another spellbook as if each spell were a scroll.

- **Oh, I know**. The amulet grants you the ability to identify magical items and cast Read Magic twice per day.

- **Better at this.** When needing to perform an intelligence check, you get a bonus +1.

Arm of Naguib

Non–Spellcasters – Medium (from Wondrous & Perilous Treasures vol.1)

This powerful magical-mechanical arm is a rarity and designed to replace someone's arm if lost or rendered infirm. It will bind to them.

- **Flex it**. The wielder receives +1 strength.

- **Packs a punch**. Able to deliver a punch for 1d4+1 damage.

- **Armed and dangerous**. The arm is able to retract the hand it comes with and draw in the hilt of a sword, mace, or other single-handed weapon. This gives a superior grip, and a bonus +1 to hit and damage. Also, the wielder cannot be disarmed of the weapon.

- **Need a hand**? The arm is able to retract the hand and install a replacement hand, including the Hand of the Spider (see W&P Treasures volume 1).

- **Feelings? Maybe**. The wielder is able to feel what the arm and its hand come into contact with but are also able to turn this off with a thought. These arms are unaffected by all but the most extreme heat and cold.

- **Anti-Magic**. Unless the arm has been damaged, its uniquely designed casing makes it unaffected by anti-magic.

Broach of Warmth and Grounding

Any - Medium

Within the crystal face of the broach are flecks of ruby, sapphire, and a strange white stone. It provides the wielder with a sense of serenity and warmth and the following benefits when wearing it:

- **I fear not the cold.** When hit with cold or ice damage, if you make your saving throw, you take no damage. If you fail, or there is no save, damage is reduced by half. The sapphire flecks will shine brightly, potentially drawing attention from those within 10'.

- **I fear not the heat.** When hit with fire or heat damage, if you make your saving throw, you take no damage. If you fail, or there is no save, damage is reduced by half. The ruby flecks will shine brightly, potentially drawing attention from those within 10'.

- **Sure footed.** When standing on a slippery surface, including magical ice, you are sure footed. If a dexterity check is required, you have a +2 bonus.

Coin of Devouring

Any – Low – Twisted (from Wondrous & Perilous Treasures vol.1)

This ordinary-looking coin was created as the last act of a vengeful apprentice who saw his Wizards' guild burned to the ground and its members killed by a greedy king who demanded just two more coins than the guild could afford to pay in new taxes.

When this coin is left with other coins unobserved, it will consume them at an alarming rate without changing its own size or weight.

- **All looks the same**. The coin manages to make itself look like the coins around it, including taking on scratches, stamps, etc.

- **Munchy**. A single *Coin of Devouring* can consume up to 50 coins per minute, up to a maximum of 10,000 coins at which point it becomes dormant for up to a week and starts again.

Gauntlets of the Ice Demon Kofnar

Any - Legendary

These are made of a combination of metal and ice, with sharp, jagged pieces sticking out menacingly. Etched throughout them are tales of the ancient ice demon Kofnar and their disciples.

- **Evil Infused.** When wearing the gloves, you view the world differently. You are more paranoid, more suspicious, and look at everything through the lens of what's in it for you. You're motivated to do things that lift you up and pushes others down or does them harm, even allies.

- **Freeze.** You are able to shoot a stream of icy magic at a target up to 50' away. If they fail a Save vs Breath Weapon, they are frozen (paralyzed) for 1d4+1 rounds.

- **Icy thrust**. You are able to create blades of ice from your gauntlets, up to three feet long. They last for a round, inflict 2d6 damage, and require a to hit roll (giving +2 to hit).

- **Icy entangle**. You are able to attempt to freeze the feet of opponents within a 30' radius of you, up to three times per day. A successful

Save vs Breath Weapon allows them to avoid it. Failure means they are stuck in place for 1d4 rounds.

- **Immunity**. You are immune to heat, fire, ice, and cold damage.

- **Walls of protection**. You are able to cast Wall of Ice up to three times per day.

- **Sense good.** The gauntlets allow you to passively detect good within 90'.

Gloves of Spider Fingers

Rogue, Warrior – Low (from Wondrous & Perilous Treasures vol.1)

These tight-fitting gloves are covered with tiny hairs that come to life. The magical gloves enhance thieving skills for the wearer or grant thieving skills if they do not have them.

- **You drive me up the wall.** Wearer gets a +25% chance when climbing walls or a 50% if they do not have the skill. For other systems, +1 to Dex when attempting.

- **Oh, shiny.** The wearer gets a +15% chance for picking pockets or a 15% chance if they do not have the skill. For other systems, +1 to Dex when attempting.

- **Knock, knock.** The wearer gets a +10% opening locks or a 10% chance if they do not have the skill. For other systems, +1 to Dex when attempting.

- **There you are.** The wearer gets a +10% to find and disarm traps but no skill if they do not have it. For other systems, +1 to Int when attempting.

Long Sword of Solonark

Warrior – High

This weapon is majestic, though heavy, made of a strange stone and weighing three times that of a regular long sword. Holding it gives a tremendous sense of responsibility.

- **Responsibility to the small.** You are unable to turn away from helping children and must intervene.

- **Detect Life.** Once per day, you are able to Detect Life within 90' and tell whether or not they are wounded.

- **Formidable**. The sword grants +2 to hit and damage, +3 versus undead.

Mace of Plant Disruption

Divine - Medium

With a black metal core and green-purple bark covering it, this mace immediately makes those who like plants, or are plant-based, uncomfortable.

- **Hits hard.** +2 to hit and damage, double damage against plants and plant-based creatures.

- **Not for me.** Immune to entanglement and plant-related spells.

Orb of Light

Spellcaster, Divine - Low

This smokey crystal ball is often found sitting in a bowl or other piece of furniture created to house it. When held, it allows the wielder to give it commands.

- **Illuminate.** The orb can project light, as per the spell, up to three times a day for up. It will last up to 1 hour during which it can either be held or float three feet off the ground. If covered, or after one hour, it will lower to the ground.

- **Detect living**. Twice a day the orb can be used to detect living creatures within 60 feet.

Orb of the Undead

Spellcaster - Low

This ebony sphere fits in a human hand and has a ghostly white streak that snakes through it. When held by a spell caster, it allows the following abilities:

- **Speak with Undead**. Twice per day the wielder is able to compel a skeleton, zombie, or ghoul to talk with them for up to 2 minutes. The range is 10 feet. The undead cease any hostilities in order to speak with the wielder but if attacked, are immune to the orb's effects.

- **Hide from Undead.** One per day, the wielder is able to hide their presence (and those within a 10′ radius) from skeletons, zombies, and ghouls for up to 1d4 turns.

Pin of the Paranoid

Any, Medium (from Wondrous & Perilous Treasures vol.1)

Long ago, a secret society known as the Parano wove their way into the courts and parliaments of many nations in the far west. Their agents and assassins were little more than whispers and the little that was written about them only contained one shred of truth, the magic that protected them was so well-crafted, so well-designed, that it could be found on the head of a pin.

These are sometimes found as a hair pin, a tie pin, or even a slim brooch.

- **Undetectable**. The wearer is unable to be detected and scried through magical means, for example spells and spell-effects like clairaudience, clairvoyance, locate object, and detection spells have no effect on them.

- **Shh, I'm creeping**. Gives the wearer the ability to move silently as if a thief of the same level.

- **Back in a minute**. 3x day, the wearer is able to blip out of existence for 1d10 minutes, then reappear exactly where they disappeared from. When they reappear, they are immediately aware of everything that transpired within 60' in their absence.

Ring of the Underdog

Any - Low - Cursed (from Wondrous & Perilous Treasures vol.2)

This ring has a sense of balance and justice all its own and seeks to nudge the odds in the direction of balance. It only affects combat.

- **Odds are against me**. When you are in combat, if your party's total level is less than the total hit dice of your foes, you get a +1 to your AC and +1 to hit until the odds are even.

- **Odds are with me**. When you are in combat, if your party's total level is greater than the total hit dice of your foes, you get a -1 to your AC and -1 to hit until the odds are even.

- **Last legs**. When you are in combat, if the *Odds are against me* applies, you can heal yourself 1d8 hit points up to twice per day.

- **Cursed**. You need a *Remove Curse* spell to remove this ring.

Short Sword of the Flame

Rogue, Warrior - High

This sword is made of a fine steel. Its hilt is encased a strange, white stone and the blade has a ruby red insert that goes from the hilt to the tip of the blade.

- **Light the way**. You are able to make the sword burst into an illuminating flame at will. This can light up an area up to 30 feet around you. The flame works as does a torch, meaning it can be used to set things on fire.

- **Well suited for battle**. The blade provides you a +2 to hit and +2 damage, as well as 1d6 additional fire damage against opponents affected by fire or heat.

- **Very well suited**. The blade has higher bonuses to hit and damage against certain creatures: +3 vs ice and cold creatures, as well as trolls and tree-folk.

- **Protect my soul and being**. The blade gives you a +1 on Saving Throws versus magical and natural fire.

Skull of Krossis

Any - Medium - Cursed

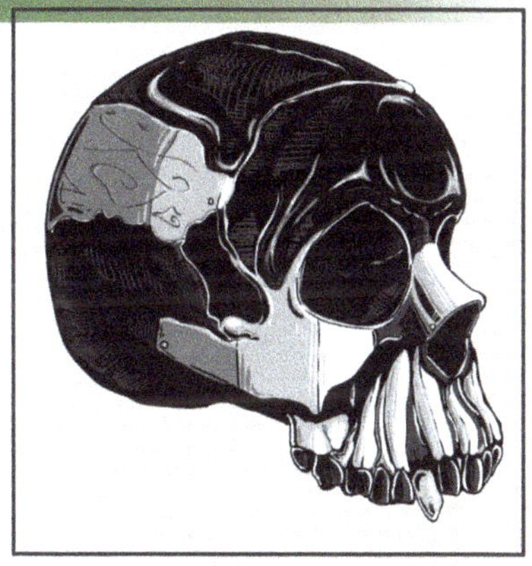

Forged to teach the greedy a lessen, these black and gold skulls are notorious for being left near dungeon treasure rooms or magical laboratories.

Once the skull is picked up, the individual finds themselves convinced they have found something of far greater value than anyone could possibly understand. They believe they hear the voice of Fortune itself, telling them that now all that lies ahead for them is greatness and they should not allow others to take it from them.

Possessing the skull results in the following effects:

- *Distracted*. You have a -1 penalty to hit and damage.

- *Eats at me*. Heal 1 less hit point per die of healing.

- *Heavy*. It weighs 20 pounds, but has the effect of being double.

- *Mine*. A Remove Curse spell is needed to separate you from the skull.

Tome of the Charming Smile

Any - High

This book has an enchanting appearance with gold buckles and a red, velvety cover. Those that commit a day to reading its secrets find themselves far more charming, and the book far less attractive as its magic spent.

- Winning smile. After studying the book for a day, you permanently gain +1 charisma to a maximum of 20.

Wand of Chains

Magical - Medium (from Wondrous & Perilous Treasures vol. 2)

This wand looks like a foot-long piece of stiff chain with a one-inch-long metal cylinder on the end. Many would ignore it, thinking it to be junk from some dwarven or gnomish machine, but what a treasure they would be missing.

- **Binding chains.** Three times per day, you can activate the wand to conjure ethereal chains that attempt to bind a creature within 30 feet. The target must succeed on a Save vs Paralysis (Strength) or be immobilized for 1d4 rounds.

- **Chain whip.** You can transform the wand into a magical flail and use it. It can extend to strike opponents up to ten feet away and has a +1 to hit and does 1d6+1 damage. It can only strike one opponent at a time.

- **Chain barrier.** Once per day, you can create a wall of interlocking chains up to 20 feet long and 10 feet high, which lasts for 1d4 rounds. It acts as a physical barrier and can be climbed with a successful strength check.

Player Map

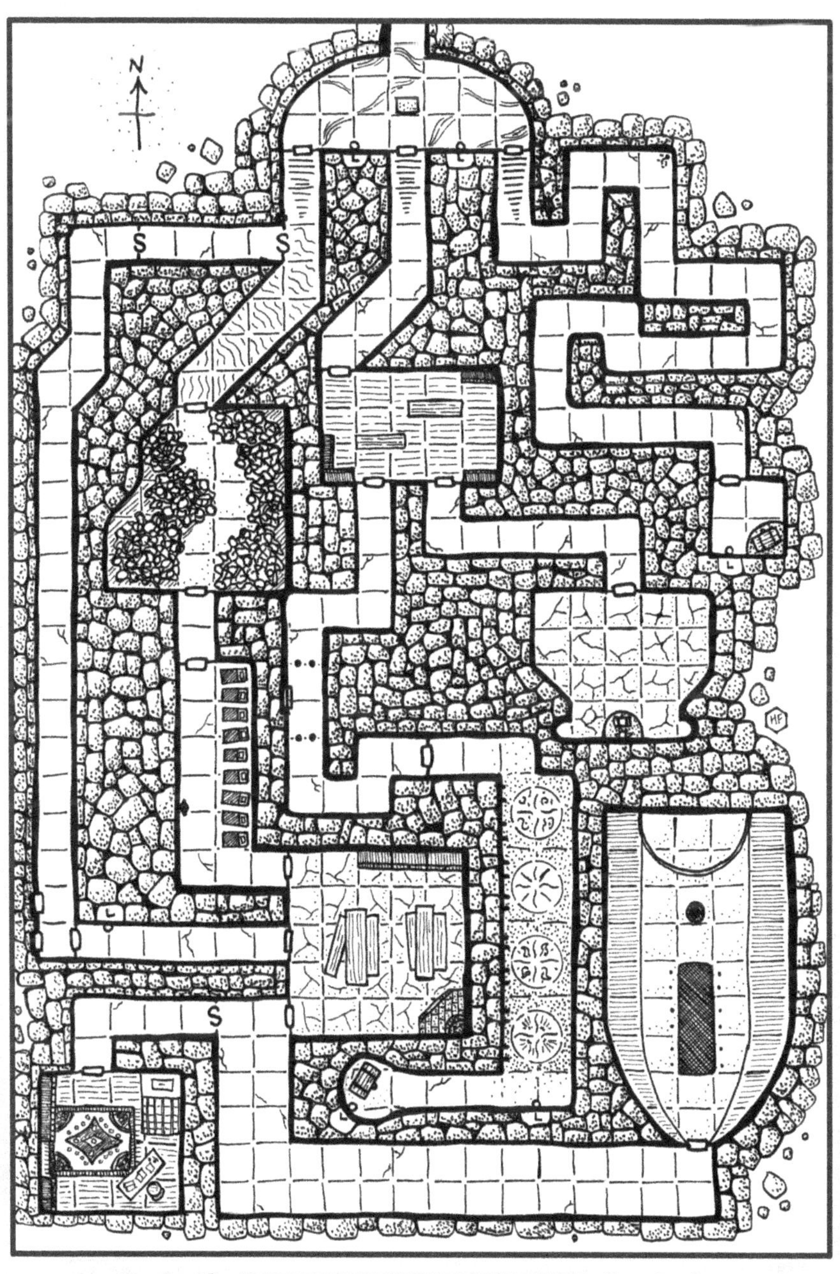

More by Adam Dreece

Over 110 new magical items to bring
trust issues and fun to your table.
Includes magical garments, assistive
magical items, and more.

AdamDreece.com

More than 120 new magical items to thrill and chill your campaign. Among other types of magical items, this volume includes furniture and items for animals.

Adventure awaits!

Whether its diving into an ancient crypt to stop the plans of an evil goblin sorcerer, or wading through a haunted swamp in search of a legendary cannon, discover our series of great adventures.

Coming Soon

Wondrous & Perilous - Tales

A collection of fantasy short stories with playable material for your own campaigns.

Coming to Kickstarter.

More Adventures!

Stay tuned for more W&P Adventures, from temples and dungeons to castles and lairs.

Treasures - Volume 3!!

What more can lurk in the imagination of Adam Dreece? Plenty. Another volume of carefully crafted magical items will be coming! This time, with magical foods and herbs.

Coming to Kickstarter.

Don't miss out.

Join the newsletter

Connect on social media

AdamDreece.com

Books by Adam Dreece

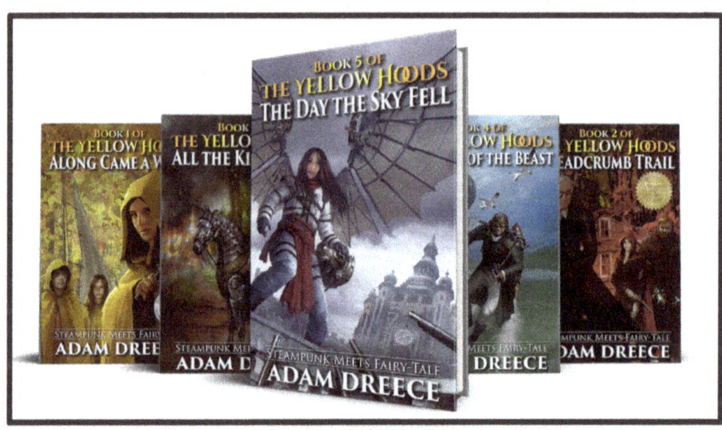

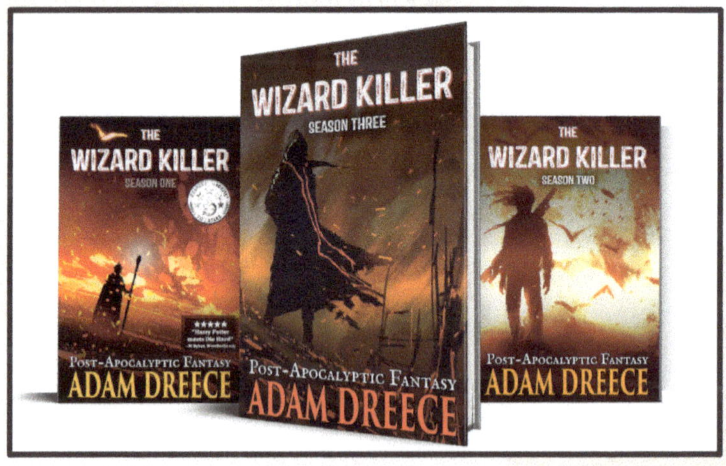

Final Word

Stay up to date with what's happening, what's going to happen, or say hi. Here's where you can find me:

- Bluesky @adamdreece.bsky.social
- Facebook /AdamDreeceAuthor
- Instagram @AdamDreece
- TikTok @AdamDreece
- Email: adam@adamdreece.com

You can also join my newsletter: adamdreece.com/newsletter

9 781988 746487